THE POWER OF PRAYER

LORANA HOOPES

 Created with Vellum

DEDICATION

Dedication Page:

The Power of Prayer is dedicated first and foremost to my grandmother who chose life when she was pregnant with my mother even though she was informed she might not survive delivery. My grandmother lived until I was four.

To my mom and dad: thank you for editing and adding your two cents. Most importantly, thank you for raising me in a Christian home and encouraging me to write.

To my husband and my children: thank you for allowing me to spend time working on this in the evenings.

To Ryann Woods: thank you for your tough questions about God. You were my inspiration for Lexi, and I'll keep praying for you.

To Kathryn and Beth: thank you for your support and feedback.

NOTE FROM THE AUTHOR

Thank you so much for picking up this book. I hope you enjoy the story and the characters as they are dear to my heart. If you do, please leave a review at your retailer. It really does make a difference because it lets people make an informed decision about books. Below are the other books in this series. I would love for you to check them out. I'd also like to offer you a sample of my newest book. Free Sample!

The Heartbeats series:
   Where It All Began

When Hearts Collide

A Past Forgiven

a past
forgiven

A Heartbeats University Romance

LORANA HOOPES

CHAPTER 1

$\mathcal{I}$ checked the diamond studded watch on my left wrist for the fourth time and sighed in annoyance. Only two minutes had passed since the last time, but I couldn't keep my eyes from returning to the classic timepiece. I had been planning this day for the last year, and Shaina's delay was disintegrating my perfectly laid plans.

"Where is she?" The agitation spilled into my voice, and my mother's brow furrowed in the mirror behind me. My mother had never understood my need for lists and order; she preferred going with the flow, which had never been my strong suit.

"I'm sure she'll be back any minute." Her voice was calm and soothing, but she couldn't hide the flicker of doubt that crossed her eyes or the furtive glance she shot at the door. Something was definitely not right. "I'll go check."

As if on cue, a knock sounded at the door, and Shaina, my best friend and maid of honor, poked her blond head in the changing room.

Shaina and I had met in college and become friends our Junior year because Shaina had been just as driven as I was.

She had been fierce competition for the top spot in class, but I had welcomed the challenge and only gloated a little when I had won, if only by a tenth of a point.

Relief flooded my body. Surely Shaina had taken care of whatever the problem was. "Is everything ready?"

"Well, sort of." Shaina's brow furrowed and her whitened teeth bit her perfectly pink bottom lip. She shuffled into the room past my mother, who took the chance to exit, closing the door behind her.

"What do you mean sort of?" A knot appeared in my stomach as I whirled to face Shaina. This could not be happening. "Did that photographer flake out on us? I knew we shouldn't have hired him. I thought he seemed flighty. I mean what kind of photographer has his studio in a garage for goodness sake? Or is it the food? I told Daniel the shop we ordered it from seemed a little dirty but he insisted on them because he *loves* their food . . ."

Shaina held up her left hand; her right stayed conspicuously behind her back. "No, the photographer is here, and the food is fine." Her eyes darted around the room, focusing on anything except my face. That was not a good sign. Shaina was terrible at hiding information and even worse at sugar coating. It was a characteristic I normally loved about her. "It's uh . . . it's Daniel; he's . . . uh . . . he's not coming."

The knot intensified, threatening to choke off my breath. My hand flew to my chest as the first signs of a panic attack coming on began. I hadn't had one in ages, but my fiancé not showing up to his own wedding would certainly be cause for one. "What do you mean he's not coming? Has he been in an accident? Is he in the hospital?"

"No, Callie." Shaina lowered her eyes and brought her hidden hand forward. She turned her palm up and offered up the cell phone it held.

I snatched the phone and swiped the screen to turn it on. Daniel's message still glowed on the screen.

-Tell Callie I'm sorry, but I can't marry her-

What does he mean he can't marry me? This had to be some kind of joke. My shoulders slumped forward, and my knuckles holding the phone turned white. "That's it? That's all? What does this mean? What am I supposed to tell everyone out there?" There were nearly two hundred people waiting in the sanctuary.

Shaina lowered her head, unable to meet my eyes and bit her lip again.

My eyes narrowed to slits as I crossed the room and grabbed Shaina's arm, eliciting a yelp of either surprise or pain. I didn't know which, and at that moment, I didn't care. "What aren't you telling me?" Her eyes narrowed to slits. "There's someone else, isn't there? Who is it? If you know Shaina, then you have to tell me."

When Shaina lifted her head, tears glistened in her eyes. "I'm so sorry, Callie."

I dropped my arm and stared at Shaina. *She's sorry? What does she have to be sorry for? It's not like her fiancé just left her. It's not like*—Anger flared up in me as the realization set in. The world flashed red, and my nostrils flared. A vice grip squeezed my heart as the loathing flooded my body. *I'll kill her. I'll strangle her with my bare hands*. My hands curled into fists and my lip quivered even as my words came out more a snarl than a statement. "You? How could you?"

Shaina shrunk under my glaring eyes and took a step backwards. Her shoulders curled inward, and her head dropped. "I didn't mean to, honest." Her words tumbled together, spilling out of her mouth as her hands wrung together. "We spent so much time together planning the wedding while you were working. It was one time, and I had no idea he had feelings for me until this morning when he called. I even tried to talk him out of leaving you."

"You?? And Daniel??" Flashes of black dotted my vision. "Were you ever going to tell me?" *You little* -- My knees began to tremble from the rage boiling inside, and I fought for control of them as my carefully laid plans crumbled around me.

Shaina turned away, her voice higher than normal. "Um, no? I was pretty sure he thought it had been a mistake, so I was going to try and forget him for your sake."

My nails dug holes into my palms, and the vein in my throat pulsed. I could almost see my heart beating. "For my sake?" The words were soft, deadly. "Shouldn't you have thought about my feelings before you slept with my fiancé?"

Shaina flinched as my words pierced like an icy dagger. "I never meant for it to happen. If you hadn't been so busy --"

My body tensed, shaking. "Don't you dare make this my fault," I seethed through clenched teeth. "I trusted you. I trusted him, and yet while trying to move up in my career you both threw that trust away."

Shaina's shoulders dropped, and she stared at her feet, her voice losing its power. "That's part of the problem, Callie; your career always came first. You couldn't even plan your own wedding. How do you think that made Daniel feel when you could never be there?"

"Get out; get out now!" Unable to contain the rage any longer, I grabbed a nearby glass of water from a small table and hurled it at Shaina. Shaina ducked and the glass missed cutting her face, but the resulting explosion of shards as the glass shattered against the wall mirrored my feelings and brought a smidgen of satisfaction. "Go be with MY fiancé and have a great life, but don't ever contact me again. I never want to see you, either of you, again."

Shaina cowered in the doorway, hands covering her face, tears spilling down her cheeks. "I am sorry Callie, and I hope someday you forgive me."

As the door closed behind Shaina, my knees finally gave out, and I collapsed on the floor. How could this happen to me? This was supposed to be my perfect day, the day I had dreamed of since I was eight years old.

An ugly, wretched sound escaped my mouth, and before I could stop them, more sobs poured out. My shoulders rose and fell as if pulled on strings by some sadistic puppet master. Darkness began to claw into the sides of my vision, and my throat closed up. My hands pulled at my throat, desperate for a little more air.

The door opened and closed. I vaguely registered my mother as she entered the room, scooped me up, and rocked me like she had when I was young. As she caressed my hair, she whispered a prayer, and for once I didn't stop her. "Please God, please heal her pain."

CHAPTER 2

*A*s the beeping intensified, I threw the alarm across the room to shut it up and pulled the pillow over my head. I had no desire to go to work today. It had been much nicer sitting in the dark yesterday feeling sorry for myself.

Though I could tell myself no one would know, I had little doubt that everyone at work would know by now that I had been stood up. They'd probably be happy. For once, I wanted to curse my braggadocios attitude and constant need to appear superior. If I hadn't made such a big deal about the wedding and invited nearly everyone in the office to it, then I might have been able to pretend the jilting never happened and go on about life. It wasn't like I had close friends at the office anyway, more like associates that I only spoke to between the hours of nine and five. But no, I'd had to brag about how amazing it was going to be and now everyone would know of my humiliation.

Sighing, I slammed my palms down on the bed. *No, I can't let him win. I have to at least act like it didn't bother me. Besides, they're announcing Junior Partner this week and if I don't show up, I'll never get the promotion.* Lowering the pillow from my face, I blinked at the intruding sunlight, and threw back the covers.

With the last reserve of energy, I rolled off the bed and stalked into my closet. A myriad of designer clothing crammed the closet, but I saw none of it. Instead, I yanked on the first black skirt and white top my hands touched. I should have wanted to make a good impression, to prove that I was doing fine, but I couldn't muster the energy.

The image staring back at me from the mirror was cringeworthy. Dark patches circled my normally bright green eyes, and they looked dead and void of life. I looked like I'd gotten punched in the face. *Better do something about those.* It was one thing not to care about my outfit, but I couldn't go in looking shabby and beat up. Grabbing some concealer, I placed a few dots under my eyes and rubbed it in. The look wasn't much better, but it would have to do. I ran a quick brush through my long dark hair that normally flowed in gentle waves, but as I hadn't showered in two days, it now hung limp and lifeless. Sighing, I pulled it into a lackluster bun, and decided "good enough" would do, for today at least.

I grabbed a quick cup of coffee and a banana and headed to work. The closer I got to work, the more the unease bubbling in my stomach grew.

By the time I parked the car and stood outside the building that served as my second home, I had to fight the urge not to turn around, go home, and crawl under my sheets again. Would everyone be talking about me? Would I have to fake my way through looks of pity all day? The very thought sounded worse than a root canal at the dentist, but somewhere deep inside a spark of courage flickered, and I grabbed ahold of it. Squaring my shoulders, I gripped the door handle to Schuster and Tuck, my firm's office, took a deep breath, and pulled it open.

Linda, the receptionist, lifted her hand in a wave and then returned her focus to her phone call. Everyone else seemed engrossed in their tasks as well. Not one eye stared at me. That could mean no one knew or that no one cared enough to make a big deal of it. The knot in my stomach untangled slightly, and my shoulders relaxed a smidgen. Maybe this wouldn't be so bad after all.

With my head held high and with deliberate braver-than-I-felt steps, I covered the distance of the lobby. I was feeling good until I turned down the hallway that led to my desk, and then I sighed. I had spoken too soon. Tina stood at her desk, staring at me with sympathetic doe-brown eyes. Ignoring them, I pulled my shoulders even farther back and marched to desk.

Tina had been my assistant since I started at the firm a few years ago, and while she was professional, I often found her overly sensitive about things.

"Are you sure you're okay?" Tina's voice oozed concern, accentuating her southern drawl. Her voice had often irritated me, and I had worked hard to break my own accent. "We're all so sorry about what happened."

Stiffening, I rolled my eyes. *Of course I'm not okay. What kind of a question is that? My fiancé left me on our wedding day for Pete's sake.* "Good news sure travels fast," I said instead, forcing a tight-lipped smile. "At least I have more time for work now, right?"

Tina's return smile would have appeared condescending coming from anyone else, but I had known her long enough to know that even with all her faults, one things she prided herself on was honesty. She held out my messages. "Sure; maybe it will even influence the partner position." Her eyes broke contact with those words, and I knew she didn't believe them, but she was saying them in hopes of making me feel better.

I flipped through the messages, my foot tapping against the floor – one of my nervous gestures. "I don't understand it, though. How could I have missed the signs?"

Tina's lips pinched together, and she looked down at her lap.

"What?" I leaned back, folding my arms across my chest. My lips drew into a tight single line as I waited for her to say the dreaded "I knew" words.

"Well, I never thought it was my place, but Daniel always seemed . . . what's the word I want? He always seemed too focused."

"Too focused? How is that a bad thing?" I thought about my recent past. Sure, I had skipped a few family occasions, but ever since my mother and father had split, they weren't as much fun anyway. My father was always off with his new wife and kids. He had tried, for a time, to see me on weekends when I was young, but once he married his girlfriend, I had gotten lost in his priorities and rarely seen him after that. My mom had been my best friend growing up, at least until she started going back to church. Now, all she ever talked about was what the church was doing and how God was working in her life. I had no time for someone I couldn't see or hear, so our relationship had grown distant.

Tina's toe ground into the floor as she mumbled the words, "Well, it seemed like he cared more about his own work than what really matters sometimes."

His work? Heat flooded my body, and my hands clenched, crumpling the messages. "It seems he cared even more about my best friend than his work." I paused, mentally forcing myself to calm down and relax my hands. A deep breath completed the outward transformation. "Anyway, it's done, and now I have more time to focus on my career. Who needs a man anyway?"

Tina nodded, timid as a mouse, and returned to her work.

I stepped into my office and sat down at the familiar, mahogany desk. A mountain of manila folders stared back at me. I drummed my fingers on the desk, hoping the monotony of the familiar would take control, but all I could do was stare at the pile.

Thoughts of Shaina and Daniel flooded my mind, constricting my throat and making it difficult to swallow. What were they doing right now? Was she cuddling with him as I used to? Was he nuzzling her neck finding that sweet spot in between her collar bones and the curve of her throat? The beep of the office phone intercom interrupted my nightmare, and I jumped.

"Yes, Tina?" I said, punching the intercom button.

"There's a Lexi on the phone for you."

Lexi? She was more of an acquaintance than a friend. I had met Lexi in college, but she had always been into partying, which had never fit in my perfect plan. Right now though, letting loose sounded like a nice diversion from the torturous thoughts of Daniel and Shaina. "Put her through."

"Callie, I'm so sorry about what happened," Lexi began. I ran my hand across my forehead. Maybe this had been a bad idea. Her overly sympathetic tone made her sound like a valley girl, which only increased my irritation, "but I know how to cheer you up. My brother's band is playing downtown tonight. Come with me to hear them. I guarantee you will have a good time."

This wasn't the first time Lexi had invited me out. In fact, I was surprised Lexi was still trying as I never bothered to come up with a good excuse when I turned her down. How many times had I told Lexi I was working late or getting a massage when I was really going home and curling up with a good book or with Daniel? Daniel, ugh. I needed a distraction from Daniel.

"Sure, that sounds like fun," I said, pushing the thought of Daniel out of my mind. It actually sounded about as much fun as watching golf on TV, but at least I wouldn't be alone, and it would get Lexi off my back.

"Really? I mean that's great," Lexi stammered in surprise. "Okay, let's meet at the Blue Banjo at eight."

"I'll be there." I hung up the phone and rubbed my temples. Would this day ever end? No answer came, and as the mountain of paperwork continued to mock me, I picked up the top folder to begin the tedious research. "Junior Partner cannot come fast enough."

When five o'clock rolled around, there were still a few folders on the desk. A week ago, I would have stayed until they were all done, but I had promised to meet Lexi tonight and surely one more day couldn't hurt. Clicking off the computer and then the light, I enjoyed the blessed darkness for a moment before heading home.

Though I normally had no trouble throwing outfits together, I stood in a pile of discarded clothes liking nothing. Nothing seemed to say 'my fiancé just left me for my best friend so leave me alone.'

Deciding I needed something to draw the attention away from my vacant eyes, I grabbed my green cowl-necked shirt. As I tugged it on over my head, I wondered if I would ever feel normal again.

A hand swipe down my jeans sent a piece of lint flying into the air. I watched it fall, realizing my life now felt a little like that, blown off course and subject to whatever force came near it.

Out of habit, I glanced over my shoulder for Daniel, who

was always ready before me. He usually stood by the door, phone in hand as he made business deals while waiting. He wasn't there, but his jacket was, hanging on the hook, taunting me. He must have left it the last time he was here, stupid jacket. I wondered what else of his might be lying around and realized tomorrow I would have to do a thorough sanitizing of the place to get rid of all his things.

Grabbing my keys, I stalked out the door, determined to have a good time and forget about Daniel.

"*A*nother round," I hollered at the blond waitress who ambled past us on the dance floor. The lights flashed, and music flooded my body, relaxing the tense nerves that had taken root. The noise filled my brain, allowing me to forget about Daniel, for the time being.

Lexi's slender body moved to the beat, her blond hair flowing against her bare shoulders. "Wow, no offense, Callie, but I can't remember the last time you were this fun to be with."

"Me either." I lifted my hair to relieve the sweat trickling down my neck, and a pair of hands, not my own, landed on my hips. They were tan, strong hands, and no ring marred them.

Twisting my body to see who the hands belonged to, I hoped for someone handsome. If I was lucky, maybe it would be someone who could make me forget Daniel for a night.

The face that met mine did not disappoint. Bright blue eyes above an impish grin stared back at me. Taut muscular arms extended from what was likely an equally chiseled chest. Yes, he could do. Desire flooded my veins, and my eyes roamed over the rest of him. The hint of a tattoo peeking out of his shirt sleeve gave him the air of a typical "bad boy," and tonight I wanted to be a "bad girl." I locked my arms around his neck, pulling him closer so the rhythm of his hips could match mine. He flashed a sexy grin and tightened his grip on me.

He leaned his head down, lips brushing my ear as he whispered, "My name is Brent, and I think you're hot."

Inwardly, I cringed at the pedantic come-on, but tilted my head back and smiled anyway. *Handsome, though not eloquent; I guess I could do a lot worse.* I ran my fingers through his short blond hair and let my mind go blank. One dance turned to into two, then three, and the rounds of Tequila kept coming.

"It must be late." My words slurred, and I realized too late that I had had too much to drink. Though we sat at a table on the side of the dance floor, the room still spun. I put my hands to my temple in hopes of stopping the roller coaster I seemed to be on, but it was no use

"I think you're right," Lexi stammered, equally inebriated, "and I have to work tomorrow, so I'm heading out." She stood and then grabbed the tabletop to keep from toppling.

"Are you okay to drive?" Brent offered his hand to steady her, and I wondered briefly how he seemed so sober. Hadn't he had as many drinks as we had? I tried to think back in my mind, but the exertion increased the pounding, and so I stopped.

"No, but my brother is." She pointed an unsteady finger to the stage where the musicians were packing up their instruments. "He can drive me."

I tried to focus on Lexi, but I wasn't sure whether the left or the right Lexi was the real one. I had always thought people were full of it when they said they were seeing double, but now I realized I had just never been drunk enough. "Thanks for getting me to come out. We should do it again soon."

Lexi flicked a sloppy salute and stumbled off.

Brent turned his attention back to me and brushed a curl from my face. "How about I drive you home?"

His fingertips felt nice on my face, soothing. I nodded, my eyes already trying to close for the night. The image of my warm apartment and soft bed called to me, but then the jacket flashed in my mind. I couldn't go home and face the jacket. My eyes flew open, and my lips parted. Leaning into Brent, I placed a hand on his solid chest, "How about you take me back to your place instead?"

Brent licked his lips, and his eyes roved my body, "I thought you'd never ask." He placed a hand on either side of my face and brought his lips down on mine. It was a rough kiss and his stubble scratched my chin, but I didn't care. Wrapping my arms around his neck, I surrendered to the feeling, or lack thereof, and leaned farther into him.

When we parted, I thrust my car keys into one of his hands and grabbed the other, stumbling after him to my red mustang parked around the corner.

The cool, night air woke me enough to acknowledge the tiny seed of doubt sprouting in my head. This wasn't like me. I was no prude, but I didn't go home with men I didn't know. I wasn't even intimate until we had both said, 'I love you.'

Shivering, I pressed my lips together, fighting the urge to call it all off. I wanted to be bad tonight. I needed to feel attractive again. Before any words could form, we were in the car; the warmth enveloped me; and I stopped caring. My eyes closed as I leaned against the leather seat.

"Come on." His voice cut through my sleepy fog. He had parked, but I had no idea where we were or even how far we had driven from the club. Tiny alarm bells sounded in my head, but I couldn't focus on them. He stood outside the car door, a hand held out to me.

I placed my hand in his, struggled to stand, and fell

against him. His chest was indeed chiseled, masculine. He spun me around and pulled me to his side, wrapping his arm around me to help me walk. We crossed the parking lot and then he deposited me against a wall while he rummaged for his keys.

The sound of silence crept in on me, stirring a little more awareness into my head. "Why is it so quiet?"

He cocked his head at me, "It's two in the morning. Everyone else is asleep."

"Right," I nodded, pointing a manicured finger at him, "sleep."

He pushed his door open and grabbed my hand, pulling me across the threshold into his apartment. The door shut behind me, and the click of the lock on the door registered something in my mind, but a thick fog obscured it.

Brent took my other hand as well and began walking backward, pulling me down the hall. I vaguely registered the clutter of clothes strewn about before we entered his bedroom. He spun me around and backed me to the bed until the back of my legs hit the frame, and I fell back, letting desire and fatigue take over.

"*G*o away," I moaned, throwing my hand over my face to block the bright light, but the sun filtered through the gaps of my fingers. "Ugh." My head felt like it weighed a thousand pounds as I tried to lift it. Giving up the fight, I lowered it back to the pillow and opened my eyes slowly to adjust to the light. White walls covered in Green Bay Packer paraphernalia filled my vision. Where was I? I didn't even like football.

I glanced down at the sheets – white. My sheets were purple Egyptian cotton ones. A feeling of unease ignited in my stomach, and I clutched the sheets tighter in my hands.

How did I get here? A shuffling noise grabbed my attention, and I turned, recoiling at the sight of the muscular man lying next to me. What had I done?

My audible intake of breath woke the sleeping giant, and he rolled over and smiled. "Good morning, sunshine."

I swallowed, racking my brain for his name "Um, hi--"

His blue eyes danced at my obvious discomfort. "Brent; we met at the Blue Banjo Club last night."

The events of the previous night flashed in my mind, and a soft pink blush crawled up my cheeks. "Right, and I guess we --"

"Oh, come on," he said, reaching out a finger to caress my face, "I thought you would at least remember that."

Trying not to flinch at his touch, I pulled the sheet to my neck and glanced around for a clock. "Um, what time is it?"

He rolled away a moment – there must be a clock on his side - "Ten."

I jumped. "Ten? Oh no, I am late, very, very late." I rolled off the bed, pausing for a moment as the world swam around me. When it stopped, I wrapped the blanket tighter around me, and tried to ignore the flame burning my ears.

"Call in sick," Brent patted the empty bed next to him. "We can order in and have breakfast together, right here."

"No, I can't do that," I said, agitated. "I am a candidate for Junior Partner. I can't take a day off." I rummaged in the clothes on the floor, tossing them in the air until I located my jeans and shirt, wrinkled from their time on the floor. Another few minutes of searching yielded the rest of my clothes.

"Suit yourself." He laced his hands behind his head and stretched out, as if he didn't have a care in the world.

I shot him a dirty look as I pulled on my clothes. Cringing at the thought of wearing jeans to work, I tried vainly to smooth out the worst of the wrinkles and then grabbed for where I normally kept my keys, but came up empty-handed. Of course, this wasn't my apartment.

Planting my hands on my hips, I turned to face Brent. "Where are my keys?"

"By the front door; on the table, I think." He pointed out the bedroom door.

I swallowed the knot growing in my stomach and hurried out of the bedroom and into the living room, scooping my keys off the hall table on the way. Slamming his front door behind me, I glanced around for my car, spotting it halfway across the parking lot. Hurrying across the asphalt already radiating heat, I climbed into it and turned the ignition on.

Easing out to the street, I glanced around for a point of reference, but nothing seemed familiar. *Oh, great.* I eased up to the intersection to see the cross streets. Baker and Yates? Where was I?

My jaw clenched as I whipped out my cell phone and turned on the GPS app. The low battery icon flashed eliciting a groan. *Please just last until I get to work.* I kept an extra cord in my desk drawer as my phone often needed a charge during the day, but I needed to get there first. I punched in the office address, and my heart sank another few feet; *thirty minutes? I am so dead.*

❀

"Where have you been?" Tina asked in a harsh whisper as she hurried toward me. Her brows furrowed, creating a pattern of wrinkles across her forehead and making her appear older than she really was.

I shook my head, "It's a long story." The sordid events of the previous night lay on my shoulders like a heavy blanket. What had I been thinking? Now I knew why I never had one-night stands. I felt dirty and cheap.

"Well, Mr. Reid said he wanted to see you in his office, as soon as you arrived. I've been trying to stall for you."

Her words hit like a punch in the stomach. "This can't be good; the partner position wasn't supposed to be announced until next week, and I can't see Mr. Reid looking like this."

"I have a skirt if you want to borrow it," Tina offered. "I know we aren't exactly the same size, but it might look better than jeans."

I raised an eyebrow at her. I'd known she was different, but why would anyone keep outfits at work? "Why do you keep a skirt at the office?"

"Oh, gosh, I am such a klutz that I keep a whole outfit here in case I spill on myself. I've already had to replace my replacement outfit twice."

I weighed the options. Tina was probably a size smaller than I was, but borrowing a skirt from her would be better than showing up in jeans, if it fit. "Okay, thanks."

Tina opened her right bottom drawer and handed over a simple black skirt. Tucking it in my arm, I headed to the nearest bathroom and peeled off my jeans. The skirt reluctantly shimmied up over my slim hips, but I couldn't tug the zipper up all the way. I pulled my blouse out over the skirt and turned to the mirror. The effect was still a little unkempt, but it was better than before. I rolled up my jeans and dropped them at my office before continuing down the long hall to Henry Reid's office.

*B*eads of sweat broke out on the back of my neck and trailed down my back as I pushed open his door.

His assistant looked up from her desk and wrinkled her nose. With her blond hair pulled back in an immaculate bun and her pressed black suit, she appeared impeccable – the way I normally dressed myself. My unease grew, but I squared my shoulders, portraying a confidence I didn't feel, and approached the desk.

"I'm here to see Mr. Reid. I'm Callie Green."

"Yes," her eyes traveled up and down my form. "He's expecting you." Disdain dripped from her words.

Ignoring her scorn, I crossed to the inner office door and smoothed my blouse one more time for good measure before stepping into the dark and masculine office.

His mahogany desk color was captured in the dark wall coloring and complemented by the dark mauve carpet. Various plaques and commendations hung from the walls and garnered my attention as I made my way to the dark brown chair across from his desk. Smoothing my skirt, I sat down and folded my hands in my lap.

Henry Reid met my gaze across the desk. He was the oldest of the partners. White hair circled his head, but the middle of his pate had lost its battle long ago. "Hello Callie, how are you doing?"

The truth was that I was a wreck, but I couldn't say that. "Not too bad sir, considering. I am throwing myself into my work." I forced a stiff laugh and then forced my hands, which had begun to curl into fists, to lay flat on my lap. My traitorous right index finger, however, continued to tap a pattern to the steady staccato of my accelerated heartbeat, displaying my nervousness.

"Yes, that is what I need to talk to you about." He leaned forward, "Do you remember the Mead case?"

I tilted my head and closed my eyes, reviewing the cases I had pored over yesterday. "I'm sorry sir. It isn't ringing a bell, but I still have a few files on my desk."

He cleared his throat. "That's the problem, Callie. It still WAS on your desk, and an injunction was supposed to be filed yesterday."

My heart dropped to the floor, and my shoulders curled inward under the heavy weight of the mistake. "I am so sorry sir."

"Normally, this would be an offense we fire for," Mr. Reid began. "We can't afford such costly mistakes."

I dropped my head into my hands and shook it back and forth. This couldn't be happening.

"But considering your history of success here and your recent personal event, I have convinced the board not to fire you."

I lifted my face to look at him through splayed fingers. "Thank you, sir."

"They have agreed to a one month suspension, without pay. I suggest you take a vacation, regain your footing, and come back ready to work. And Callie," he emphasized, "they won't be this lenient IF there is a next time."

"Yes sir." I gave a curt nod and then stood. The Junior Partnership flashed in my mind, and I cleared my throat, unsure of how to ask the question on my mind. "I don't suppose---" I broke off mid-sentence, unable to form the rest of the question, but he read my mind.

"I'm sorry, Callie. I couldn't recommend you this time."

My head fell. "I understand, sir."

"But there will be another junior partnership next year. If you come back refreshed and re-focused, I could recommend you then."

Another whole year? The weight of the prospect of another year of doing grunt work bore down on me, threatening to release the tears now crowding my throat. As my heart shrunk in my chest, I fought to compose myself.

"Thank you, sir." I forced a tight smile and shook his hand. Drawing myself as straight as I could manage under the heaviness descending my body, I shuffled out of the office and past the perfectly put-together, snarky assistant to the hallway.

As the door closed behind me, I pressed a hand over my mouth to hold back a sob. My eyes darted around for the bathroom sign, and I hurried to the women's room. Locking the stall behind me, I sank down on the toilet. Tears obscured my vision and tumbled down my cheeks. *What is happening to me? Why is everything going wrong? How am I going to get back on track now?*

When the tears were spent, I splashed water on my still puffy face and scuffled back to my office. My head was down, all of my bravado gone.

"Oh, no, what happened?" Tina asked. The concern in her voice nearly broke the dam holding back another flood of tears.

I swallowed and bit my lip. "I missed filing an injunction yesterday."

"Are you . . .?" Tina averted her eyes and wrung her hands together.

My head shook back and forth, "No, I've been given a one month suspension." The words tasted dirty in my mouth. Suspension? I would have never thought the words would be applied to me, the girl at the top of her class who had her whole life planned out. I swallowed the vile words to dislodge them from my throat.

"Well, that's not so bad," Tina said, touching my arm.

"It could be worse," I agreed, "but what am I going to do for a month?" The thought of sitting around my empty apartment that long chilled me to the bone. I had never been one to sit at home. In fact, in the time I had been at the firm, I had taken only one sick day.

Tina's eyes lit up, and she snapped her fingers. "Do you still have your honeymoon tickets?"

"Yes, I think the information is on my computer. Why?"

"Send it to me. I have a friend who's a travel agent. I bet he can work something out and send you to a nice place for most of that time."

A spark flickered in my dark heart. "Really? That would be great." I pulled Tina into a hug, turning her in a circle before realizing what I had done. I never hugged people and especially not people at work. Dropping my arms, I mumbled an apology.

Tina laughed, ignoring my apology. Her eyes sparkled. "I'll call him right away. Go home and rest, but be sure to have your phone on."

I didn't know how to thank Tina. Even after all the years we had worked together, I barely knew anything about her, but that was going to change. An escape to a tropical island sounded like just the thing to help me forget Daniel and focus on rebuilding my self-esteem, and I couldn't believe Tina was willing to help me. As I gathered up my things, I promised myself that I would be different when I came back and that I would pay more attention to others around me, especially Tina.

As I entered my apartment, the silence seemed almost palpable. Rubbing my neck, I looked around for some way to pass the time. A book on the coffee table garnered my attention, and I scooped it up and reclined on the brown, leather couch.

I couldn't remember the last time I had read this book, and as I had no idea what was happening in it any longer, I flipped back to the beginning. I read the first page, then read it again, and again. Sighing, I closed the book and glanced at the clock. I'd managed to kill a whopping five minutes.

Setting the book back on the small coffee table, I grabbed the remote. Maybe some mindless TV would help pass the time. A click of the power button brought the screen to life and the news filled the screen. Election coverage, ugh,

I was so over the presidential race this year. Politics had never held my attention anyway. I clicked the channel up button: soap opera, talk shows, game shows. There was nothing worth watching on TV in the middle of the day. A rerun of Friends was the only thing that seemed remotely interesting, and I soon got lost in the friendly banter of the characters.

The shrill ring of the phone broke my trance, and I snatched it up before the end of the first ring. "Hello?"

Tina laughed on the other end. "Hello? Callie? Wow, it didn't even ring on my end."

"Sorry, I seem to have no life right now," I replied, sitting forward on the couch and fingering the gold chain around my neck. It held no special appeal or sentimental value, but touching the chain often brought comfort when I was nervous.

"Well, you will soon. Can you catch a plane tomorrow?"

"Of course I can." I listened in rapt attention as Tina rattled off the details of the vacation. Twenty-one days in the Caribbean, a hotel on the beach, and all-inclusive; it sounded like heaven. I'd have to come up with a special way to thank her.

After hanging up the phone, I danced a little jig to the hall closet and opened the door, pulling out my red suitcase. It was nice to be feeling something other than dread and despair.

I threw the suitcase on the bed and began rummaging through my drawers for swimwear, tank tops, and skirts. With the bag packed, I phoned my mother for a ride to the airport the next morning and then turned to the task I was not looking forward to – gathering all of Daniel's things.

I wandered around the apartment picking up books, ties, socks – anything that was Daniel's or reminded me of Daniel – and shoving it in a box. The coat was the last item. I snatched it off the coat rack and flung it on the top of the pile to take out in the morning.

*T*he next morning, I glanced around the apartment for anything I had missed as I waited for my mother to arrive. The list on the coffee table had been checked off – the clothes were packed, the major appliances unplugged, the mail was taken care of. My eyes landed on the box of Daniel's things, and a new surge of anger flooded my body. Snatching the box up, I flung open the front door and stomped around the corner to the communal trash dumpster. I threw the whole thing in, box and all, and then wiped my hands together, feeling a smug sense of satisfaction.

The deed done, I retraced my steps and found my mother standing at my front door.

"Dare I ask?" she said, one eyebrow raised.

"Just taking out the trash," I said sweetly and stepped past her into the apartment.

"Okay," she said slowly, drawing the two syllables out in an exaggerated effect. She followed me into the apartment and tried another tactic to get me to open up. "Do you want to tell me why you're running away then? It's not as if that is going to soothe your grief."

I pulled the handle out of the rolling suitcase and rolled my eyes as I answered her. "I'm on suspension, mom; I was told to go on vacation."

"You were told to take a break and clear your head—which isn't the same thing. You know, honey, I've started praying again and that has helped clear my head."

My muscles tensed at the mention of God. I'd had no use for him before, but I certainly didn't want to hear how loving he was now, after being left at the altar. "That's great mom.

I'm glad it works for you, but I am not praying to anybody, especially to a God who cared so little about me that he let my life get so far off track. After all, if he really cared about me he could have stopped Daniel from leaving me on my wedding day or from sleeping with Shaina in the first place."

My mother's lips pursed as she shook her head. "Well, at least let me pray for you and your safety."

I checked my watch and sighed. "Fine, mom, as long as it's quick."

A look of reproach crossed her features, and she opened her mouth as if to scold me, but deciding against it, she sighed and closed her eyes. Her prayer was short, a prayer of safety, but I couldn't resist tapping my foot against the carpet. I couldn't wait to get out of Texas and go somewhere where no one knew my shameful secret, either of them.

CHAPTER 3

*S*ighing, I collapsed on the king size bed in the hotel room and flung my arms out. What a long flight! It had been just my luck lately to be seated next to an elderly man who wouldn't stop talking and didn't seem to know how to read body language. I had thought if I stuck my nose in a book or plugged in my headphones that he might get the message I wasn't interested in a conversation, but he had kept prattling away until he had finally talked himself to sleep.

Rolling over, I enjoyed the feel of the soft comforter on my skin. It wasn't a tacky flower comforter like most hotels. Instead it was some soft material in a light blue color.

The salty, fresh air wafting in the slightly open window relaxed my muscles, and the stress began to peel off my shoulders in layers. This was exactly what I had needed. I glanced up at the peach colored walls and stifled a laugh at the picture of the ocean hanging on the wall I was facing. Though it was pretty, I could hear the real thing seeping in the window.

Sitting up, I grabbed the suitcase and hefted it onto the

bed, unzipping it. My current clothes lay sticky and molded to my skin from the long plane ride, and a sniff revealed they needed a wash. A pink maxi dress and matching sandals seemed appropriate for the beach, and I slipped them on after removing my other clothes.

My hair was also flatter than I would have liked, but a few shakes gave it some body. I touched up my makeup and pulled the sliding glass door open.

The warm night air caressed my face much like Daniel's fingertips used to, and I breathed in a deep breath. This was perfect; I'd have to buy Tina lunch when I got back to Texas. Maybe Tina wasn't so bad after all.

I slid the door shut behind me and stepped onto the cream-colored sand that appeared almost white at the base of the various palm trees dotting the landscape. The palm leaves stirred slightly with the gentle breeze which also lifted my hair, swirling strands about my face. Blue water licked the sand and called to me like an old friend. *I'll have to go swimming tomorrow.* As I stepped closer to the water, I could see the colorful fish swimming back and forth in the clear, calm glass.

The soft sound of music to my right caught my attention, and I turned to see a small bar surrounded by tiki torches. A handful of people sat in the few barstools and tables and several more stood around sipping their drinks. The glow of the light pulled at me, daring me to come and join it, and since the beach area to the left was empty except for a few occupied lounge chairs, I accepted the invitation and set off to check out the scene at the bar.

Probably twenty people, who seemed close to my age, professionals at least, hovered around the bar. An iPod speaker system sat on the bar's counter playing soft reggae music that my head began to bob to.

"What'll you have?"

The voice was deep and masculine, and as I turned to find the man who owned it, a small gasp escaped my lips. Broad shoulders that had been tanned in the sun stood out against his cream tank top, and dark brown hair fell in waves to about his chin. He was probably the most handsome man I had ever seen, but it was his piercing green eyes that I couldn't seem to look away from. He stared at me expectantly, an empty glass in his hand as he waited for my order.

"Uh, tequila sunrise," I stammered as the blush climbed my cheeks. Had he heard my gasp? I tried to look away, but his gaze was a magnet drawing my eyes back to him.

"Tequila, huh?" His lips pulled into a smile revealing perfectly white teeth, and my heart fluttered in my chest.

"It's my weakness." My lips parted, and my tongue darted across my bottom lip. I wondered how his lips would feel against mine. Apparently, he was a weakness for me as well.

"In that case, how about a double shot?" The wink he flashed solidified the notion that he was flirting with me, but I couldn't tell whether that was because he liked me or because it was part of the job description.

"Sure." My heartbeat magnified in my ears, and despite his magnetic pull, I forced my attention away from the bartender and back to the crowd, hoping to hide the red on my face. Though the bartender was easily the most handsome man there, several other nice looking gentlemen filled the area. Most appeared to be chatting with women already, but one man sat alone, tapping at his laptop and nursing a beer.

"Here you go." The bartender slid a colorful glass my way.

I grabbed the drink, smiling at the tiny blue umbrella attached to the side, and reached for my bag. I froze as I realized I didn't have my bag or any cash on my person. My dress didn't even have pockets. "Um . . . any way I can charge this to my room? I forgot my purse."

"No need. It's all inclusive here." He tossed another wink at me and flashed a lopsided grin.

"Oh right. Thank you." I raised the glass in a mock salute and headed to an empty table. Smoothing my dress, I sat in the wicker beach chair and glanced around. *Why didn't I think to at least bring a book?*

The answer to my question appeared a moment later as a tall man approached the table and motioned to the empty chair across from me. "Mind if I sit down?"

I nodded once in agreement, checking him out as he folded his frame into the chair. He appeared about thirty with blond hair and blue eyes.

"So," he took a sip of his beer and raised his eyebrows suggestively at me, "What do you do?"

I fought to keep my eyes from rolling. He came across like a frat boy who hadn't quite realized he was no longer in college, but I was determined not to be judgmental and to have a good time, so I pasted a smile and answered, "I'm a lawyer, here on vacation, clearing my head."

"Lawyer, huh? That must be interesting." He leaned across the table bringing a whiff of alcohol with him. He had clearly had more than one beer already.

Forcing another smile, I leaned back, away from his breath. "Hah, that's rarely the case. TV makes it look exciting, but I do a lot of paperwork and research right now."

"Well, then I'd say you definitely deserve a break, huh?"

"You have no idea," I agreed, taking a long drink of the tequila. I was not usually much of a drinker, but the alcohol felt good as it burned down my throat.

"My name is Owen." He stuck out a large hand which I

shook after only a moment's hesitation. His hand was smooth and . . . manicured? He obviously did not do physical labor for his job.

"I'm Callie. Nice to meet you."

Owen's eyes roamed my face before beginning to slide south. Why was it that men couldn't keep their eyes focused on women's faces? "So . . . are you here with your boyfriend?"

Images of Daniel flashed into my mind, and I squeezed my eyes shut, shaking my head to clear the treacherous face. The last thing I wanted to do on this vacation was think about Daniel. "I most definitely am not."

"I'm single too," he hinted, tracing a circle around the top of his glass with his index finger. "Would you like to have dinner with me tomorrow? We could meet at the hotel restaurant here."

I opened my mouth to decline and then closed it. While he wasn't my normal type, it was just dinner. Besides, my normal type had ended up sleeping with my best friend. The fact that he seemed drunk already bothered me – I didn't need any more drunken trysts, but maybe it was his first night, and he was just relaxing. I wasn't here to psychoanalyze people, and I'd probably be enjoying more of these drinks while I was here. Besides, if dinner turned out to be a disaster, I wouldn't have to see him again.

"Sure, that sounds nice." With the words out of my mouth and unable to be recalled, I tilted back the last of my drink. Though not drunk, the jet lag, combined with the alcohol, created a soft buzzing in my head, and I excused myself before I ended up passing out on the table.

Waves of fatigue bombarded me as I opened the sliding glass door and closed it behind me. Kicking off my sandals, I crawled into the inviting bed, not bothering to change. My teeth felt fuzzy, and I knew I should get up and brush them, but the bed had wrapped its comfort around me, and I couldn't lift my head, much less my body. *I'll brush them tomorrow* was the last thought in my head before the darkness won.

he sunlight peeking in my window woke me the next morning. Yawning, I stretched out my stiff muscles and did a double take at my watch. *Nearly noon? I guess jet lag does mess you up.* This trip was my first out of the continental United States, and I'd had no idea how tired the flight over would make me. I never slept past eight am unless I was sick or drunk. I cringed as the night with Brent blazed in my memory again.

Pushing it away, I plodded out of bed and into the bathroom. After turning on the water in the tub, I slipped off my dress and stepped into the bathtub, letting the warm water energize me. When I felt thoroughly refreshed and washed, I toweled off and, wrapping the white fluffy towel like a sarong around my chest, traipsed back into the main room to pick today's outfit.

I wanted something comfortable but also eye catching, so I grabbed a green tank that brought out my eyes and a pair of shorts. After slipping them on, I ran a quick brush through my dark hair and grabbed my sunglasses. It was time to check out the rest of what the island had to offer.

The hotel itself was gorgeous, but very much like other hotels I had been to: a spa, a gift shop, and a few small restaurants sat on the premises but not much else, so I headed out of the hotel to the village outside.

The sun beat down, sending small beads of sweat trickling down my back as I traversed the walkway. I needed a hat or a fan, something to keep the blazing sun off my head.

As small shops straddled the quaint street, I approached one that was laden with clothing and begin to search through the wares. Dresses, skirts, and tops filled the tiny shop, and a dark-skinned woman sat on a stool, eyeing me and fanning herself.

My hand landed on a beautiful green, blue, and red maxi skirt that called my name, and I handed it to the lady to wrap up for me. I added a straw hat before leaving and was just about to place the hat on my head when I saw a man braiding hair a few feet ahead. I'd often pictured a braid in my hair whenever I thought of myself lounging on a beach, so I tucked the hat in the bag for now and sidled up to his stand.

He was just finishing a braid on the current customer, his skilled hands deftly weaving the hair back and forth. "How much to do one small braid in the front of my hair?" I asked, pointing to the front right side.

The dark man smiled at me as he wrapped a small rubber band around the bottom of the woman's braid. "For you, pretty lady, I take ten dollar."

The lady thanked him and smiled at me as she vacated the chair, and I handed over the ten-dollar bill I had just fished from my purse. I couldn't believe I was actually letting a stranger run his fingers through my hair, but I had to admit the feeling was rather nice.

"Blending in, are you?"

I glanced out of the corner of my eye to see the handsome bartender from the previous night. My heart fluttered in my chest. He looked just as handsome today in cargo shorts and a green t-shirt. "Uh yeah, I figured I should try some of the local culture." Why did I lose the ability to speak coherently around this man?

"Well, Sammy here is the best braider around, so you are in good hands." He clapped a hand on the shoulder of the man and flashed another charming smile.

My pulse drummed in my ears. What was it about this guy? Why did he have such an effect on me? "Are you not working at the bar today?" I hoped the question sounded nonchalant, though I feared my attraction to him was showing through.

His head tilted as he regarded me, his eyes twinkling. "I don't work here; I was covering a shift last night, for a friend."

Something in the way he answered led me to believe there was more to that story, but as he didn't seem inclined to share, I decided not to push. "What do you do then?" I asked, finally recovering the ability to string intelligible words together.

"I manage a few companies back in the states."

"Are you vacationing then?"

"I guess you could say that." That twinkle in his eye was so distracting as was his uncanny ability to give vague answers to my questions. "Listen, do you want to get some lunch after Sammy finishes your hair? I'd like to show you a fantastic, local eatery."

Yes. My heart flip-flopped, and my pulse revved, accelerating in my chest, but I took a deep breath to regain control. "I don't even know your name." I glanced up at him, and Sammy smirked.

"It's JD, and people around here can vouch for me."

"I'm Callie, but I don't know people around here so them vouching for you doesn't mean much."

"He's a good guy," Sammy interjected.

"See? I'm a good guy." JD smiled. "Come on." His bottom lip protruded in just the hint of a pout, and desire flickered in my veins again. I wanted to gently nibble on that protruding lip and then . . . I squeezed my eyes shut, stopping the tempting thoughts. What was wrong with me?

"Okay, fine, but just lunch." Of course, if it turned into something more, I wasn't sure I would be upset.

Sammy finished the braid and tied it off, and JD stretched out a hand to me. It was large and masculine, as Owen's had been, but there were also callouses. He had probably never had a manicure in his life.

I placed my hand in his, enjoying the roughness that rubbed against my smooth skin. Tingles raced up my arm at his touch, sending another flush crawling up my neck. I lowered my eyes, afraid of what he might see in them, but as soon as I was standing, he dropped my hand. My eyes shot to his face, but he was already walking on. Ignoring the empty sensation pulsing through my hand, I hurried to catch up to him.

"You aren't a vegetarian, are you?" JD asked as we strolled past various shops.

"No, I like to eat—I need the protein," I laughed, "because I work out a lot."

"What do you do?" He turned into an eatery on the left side of the street.

"I kick box."

His eyes widened, and a laugh escaped my lips. I was used to that reaction. Though athletic, my 5'7" frame did not scream 'heavy hitter.'

"I'm sorry," he said, holding up his hands in apology, "I don't know many women who kick box."

"I don't either," I agreed, though more women were joining my gym every day, "but it's the only workout that I have continued for any length of time; I've been training for ten years. I guess I get bored easily, but it's never the same workout, so it stays fresh." A furtive glance at his well-toned body sent another flame of heat across my face, forcing me to look away. "What about you? Do you work out?"

"Mainly running and lifting, but I've been known to hit a bag now and then."

Images of JD shirtless flooded my mind. I pictured the two of us in one of the small changing rooms in my gym icing each other's wounds in between stolen kisses or crawling into an Epson Salt bath together after a hard workout. My ears burned with heat, and I shook my head to clear it. What was wrong with me? I didn't even know him, and I had just warmed the bed of another man I didn't know.

Daniel. He was the reason. His leaving me at the altar had damaged my psyche and these lustful thoughts must be my way of regaining it.

The waitress approached, and I followed her, thankful that JD appeared not to have noticed my face or crimson ears. She led us to an empty table with a bright blue and orange umbrella attached to offer shade. Several similar tables sat throughout the restaurant, each with a different colored umbrella.

JD pulled out my chair, and I cocked an eyebrow at him as I sat down, unsure whether to be flattered or offended. I could pull out my own chair, but the gesture had been nice.

I picked up the paper menu and wrinkled my forehead. Everything was in Spanish. *I have no idea what any of this is, how am I supposed to pick something to eat? Okay, pollo is chicken, I remember that; thank you Ms. Alvarez. So maybe I'll order something with chicken.*

JD scanned the menu before laying it down. "Do you trust me to order for you?"

Narrowing my eyes at him, I considered his offer. Was he offering because he could sense I had no idea what to order or was he being chauvinistic and assuming I couldn't order for myself? "I thought you were here on vacation. How do you know so much about the cuisine?"

He shrugged, "I come here every year."

My eyebrow inched up my forehead. He must make a lot of money to afford a trip like this every year. While I wasn't poor, most of the money I had spent the last few years had been Daniel's. Even Junior Partners didn't make as much money as people thought. The realization that I was going to have to cut back on my spending habits when I returned home slapped me in the face. "Sure, order whatever you think will be good."

I placed the menu back on the table and removed the hat that I had donned after leaving Sammy. I placed it on the empty chair next to me as JD called the waitress over and ordered. Lifting my hair off the back of my sweaty neck, I twisted it up into a roll, so the cool breeze could the spot. With the other hand, I pushed a stray tendril behind my ear until I realized that JD was staring at me. My face flushed, and I released my hair.

JD dropped his eyes and cleared his throat. It was the first time he had appeared flustered. "So, are you seeing that guy from last night again?"

His question caught me off guard, and I leaned back in the chair and crossed my arms. It appeared I hadn't imagined his interest last night. "Were you spying on me?"

"No, just observing. I see guys like him come and go while I'm here every year. I didn't want you to get hurt."

"You don't even know me." Defensive walls shot up at his insinuation, and my arms pulled tighter to my chest. "What do you know about how I might get hurt?"

JD softened his voice, "I could see the sadness in your eyes last night. I sense that you are dealing with some pain, but guys like that won't make it go away."

"Guys like what?" I didn't know why I was arguing with him, I hadn't been that attracted to Owen, but my eyes narrowed to slits anyway as I dared him to continue.

"You know the kind I mean." He leaned back, folding his arms across his muscular chest. "Here for a week, hoping for a fling, never going to call again after that."

"Well, how do you know that isn't what I'm looking for?" It was a challenge, and I didn't even know why I was throwing it.

He considered me for a long moment, his eyes never wavered from mine.

What is he looking at? Frustrated, I broke his gaze and glanced away.

He leaned forward, propping his head on folded hands, still never shifting his eyes. "I don't think that's really what you're looking for."

I stared down at my wrists as I thought of the night with Brent again. *Maybe he's right; I can't say I'm proud of that night, but who could blame me? Still, who I see is none of his business.*

His words spurred my need to always be right and have the last word, and I raised my head, returning his stare and almost daring him to contradict me. "Well, as a matter of fact, I am seeing Owen again tonight for dinner."

Though he couldn't hide the flicker of surprise that flashed across his eyes, he managed to keep his voice even. "Ah, well, I am sure you can handle yourself, but do remember my advice."

Before I could retort, the food arrived. A colorful mix of red, brown, green and orange tantalized my eyes as the savory smell delighted my nose. My mouth watered, and I grabbed my fork, scooping up a mouthful, but JD's hand stopped my arm before it reached my mouth.

"Wait, can we pray over it first?"

"Are you serious?" I raised an eyebrow and stared at him, "You pray before you eat?"

"Of course, don't you?"

Lifting my chin, I pointed my nose in the air, "I don't pray at all; I don't believe in praying to a God who allows someone to experience intense pain."

"But you do believe in God?"

"I---" I stopped, unsure of how to answer his question. My forehead furrowed as I thought. Did I believe in God? "I don't know," I shrugged. "My mom does, and when I was young we went to church." A vague memory of entering a church, holding hands with my mother and father before they divorced flashed across my mind. "Maybe I used to."

"Well, I do believe in God, and I believe everything happens for a reason. I don't know what happened to you, but I do believe that God had a reason for whatever it was."

My body tensed as I clenched my fork, "Yeah? A reason to be stood up at the altar?"

JD cast his eyes down. "I'm sorry. That had to be painful, but yes, even in a situation like that; I think God has a plan for you."

"Well, let's agree to disagree on this point." I shook his hand off my arm and brought the fork back to my mouth. Across from me, JD closed his eyes and bowed his head but remained silent. I opened my mouth to take a bite; then sighed, put my fork down, and closed my eyes as well.

"Dear Lord," JD prayed, "Thank you for all the blessings you have bestowed upon us. Thank you for this food we are about to eat and for the hands that have prepared it. Thank you for new friendships, and Lord, please allow us to understand your reasoning regarding events that are beyond our control. Amen."

"Interesting prayer," I said, cocking my eyebrow at him when he opened his eyes. "Are you hoping that something will be revealed to me that will change my mind about who God is?"

The twinkle flared again in his eyes, and his lips formed a teasing smile, "I think it will in time."

"How could you possibly know that? You don't even know me." Why was I even continuing this conversation? I'd heard enough religious mumbo jumbo from my mother; I didn't need it from a stranger too. Yet, I couldn't muster the desire to leave. Not only was I physically attracted to him, but there was something else about him that intrigued me as well.

"Not yet, but I know God and even though I don't always know the way He works, I have seen people receive various truths from Him, and I know he works in mysterious ways that we don't always understand at first."

My gaze lingered on him a moment longer as I tried to decide if he were serious or playing me. Deciding it didn't matter for now, I returned my attention to the food and took a bite of the delicious dish, savoring the flavors that exploded in my mouth. I sneaked a glance at JD curious if he just had good taste or if somehow he knew exactly what I liked?

The rest of the meal was finished in a comfortable silence; and after lunch JD paid for the meal and escorted me back to the hotel.

"Thank you for having lunch with me," he said as they reached the front door. "I wish you well on your dinner tonight and the rest of your visit here."

He bowed slightly and before I could respond, he turned and walked back the way we had come, leaving me battling confusion over his baffling behavior.

. . .

*T*lay around the pool the rest of the afternoon pondering the time with JD. What was it about him? True, he was handsome with his toned body and tanned skin – I could picture myself enjoying being wrapped in his arms – but he was also obsessed with God, which I had no stomach for. So, why couldn't I get him off my mind? I'd probably never even see him again after leaving the Caribbean, but I couldn't shake the image of his face from my mind.

At four o'clock, I headed back to the room to shower and prepare for dinner with Owen, which I was no longer remotely excited about. For whatever faults he had, JD was right that I didn't need another man like Owen, but I had promised to go, and I didn't like reneging on my word.

I chose the new colorful maxi, which ended up hugging my hips, and a matching blue tank top I had brought with me for dinner. As I regarded the image in the mirror, I thought about changing because I didn't want to look too good and lead him on, but a check of my watch showed 6:02. Perfect. I hated being the first one when meeting people, but if I were any later, it would be rude. Exiting the room, I headed to the hotel bar to meet Owen.

The music spilled out of the restaurant before I even reached the entrance. *Well this isn't going to be the best place to have a conversation.* I scrunched my nose, coughing at the smell of cigarette smoke that permeated the air as I made my way toward the bar. Owen sat perched on a barstool, drinking a beer and surveying the crowd. His eyes lit up, and he lifted his hand in a wave when our eyes met. I took a deep breath, exhaled, and headed that direction. *It's just dinner, remember?*

"Well, hello gorgeous." He grabbed my hand and his eyes traveled my body up and down. It was a gaze that left me feeling dirty more than desirable.

The hair on the back of my neck bristled with his gaze. "Hello yourself." I flashed a tight smile and extricated my hand as politely as I could.

"Do you want a drink?"

"Sure; I'll have a Tequila Sunrise." I was going to need quite a few drinks to get through this evening.

After the drinks were ordered and poured, we made our way to a secluded booth in the back. The low lighting set a romantic air and since the booth was surrounded on three sides, only the general buzz and not specific words of the conversations around them reached my ears.

"So, why did you decide to become a lawyer?" Owen's eyes focused briefly on mine before trailing down to stare at my lips.

I placed a finger to my lips. Why had I become a lawyer? It seemed so long ago I wasn't even sure. "Well, I always loved arguing when I was younger, and TV made it look glamorous."

"Yes, it does. I bet you would be fantastic on TV." He placed his fingers on my arm and traced an imaginary pattern.

My skin crawled, and I grabbed my drink, dislodging his hand. "What about you? How did you get into . . . what do you do again?" I took a sip, but as soon as I set the drink down, his hand resumed its position.

"I sell insurance. My dad owned the company, and I joined him." He traced his fingers up my arm.

Stifling a shiver, I tried my best to ignore his hand. "You don't want to sell insurance?"

He scooted closer and laughed, "No, not at all, but the money is good, so why change?"

Something in that answer sounded so wrong, but I wasn't sure what. I loved money, too; it was one reason I had gone into law in the first place, though I wasn't at the point where

I was making good money yet. Still, money equaled power which equaled happiness, right?

"So, how long are you here for?" Owen changed the subject.

I focused back on Owen and the current conversation. "Um, I'm here for about 20 more days."

He pouted his lip, "Well, I leave in five days, but I hope we can spend a lot more time together." As he inched closer, he winked and licked his lips. Unlike the wink that JD had thrown last night in the bar, Owen's wink was leering and creepy.

"Mmmhmm," I nodded, pursing my lips together and glancing around. How long had I been here? More importantly, how much longer did I have to stay before I could leave without appearing rude? As Owen continued rattling on about his work and his hobbies, I snuck a quick peek at my watch. 6:30, *ugh I am going to need more tequila if I have any hope of staying here much longer*. I caught the waitress's eye, and motioned for another drink.

Tuning back into the conversation long enough to hear "Nascar is like the best sport," I rolled my eyes and tuned out again. *Oh Lord, does he have nothing intelligent to talk about?* I stirred the straw in my drink and thought back to the afternoon with JD. He had been so easy to talk to and had intelligent things to say. True, he was a bit of a "Bible thumper," but so was my mother and perhaps I could loosen JD up.

I jumped as Owen's hand relocated from my arm to my knee. *I don't think so mister*. Picking his hand up, I smiled and placed it back on the table. Owen never missed a beat, just kept rattling on. My second drink arrived, and I downed it, sighing as the alcohol relaxed my muscles. *Maybe Owen isn't that bad, after all. At least he's cute and I could probably shut him up easily*. The third drink arrived, and my lids grew heavy. I shook my head and took a deep breath, opening my eyes wide, but the spinning room stirred nausea in my stomach, and I blinked them closed again.

"Another round?" Owen leaned forward.

"I shouldn't," I replied, pushing my glass away.

"Oh, one more won't hurt," Owen pressured, signaling the bartender.

"No really---"

"It's no problem."

"The lady said she's had enough."

The commanding voice sliced through my fog, and I raised my head to see JD standing at the end of the table. Though the rest of the world spun, my eyes locked on his, relief coursing through my body.

"Excuse me, but we're on a date here." Owen stood, squaring his shoulders and throwing his chest out.

JD didn't take Owen's bait. Instead, he crossed his arms and returned Owen's stare. "And it just ended." His words were cool but confident. He unfolded his arms and stretched out a hand, "Callie?"

I looked from one man to the next, mumbled an apology toward Owen, and took JD's hand.

"Whatever," Owen said and stomped away.

My world tilted as I stood up, and my knees buckled. JD wrapped an arm around me, and I leaned into him, placing one hand on his chest. I closed my eyes and took a deep breath. He smelled clean and salty like the ocean. Sighing, I laid my head on his shoulder as he led me out of the bar. There was a safeness and security in his arms. I couldn't remember the last time I had felt so protected.

"What's your room number?" JD asked, shaking my shoulder.

"103," I whispered, and my eyes closed again.

"Whoa, whoa, no falling asleep yet." JD shook a little harder this time.

It was a struggle, but I managed to keep my eyes open until we got to my door.

"Key?" he prodded.

"Somewhere in there," I mumbled and held out my bag.

He rummaged in the small purse until he found the key card, inserted it, and opened the door. Taking my hand, he pulled me into the room. The light clicked on and illuminated the room.

"Thank you." I turned to face JD and fell into him, placing both hands on his chest. His muscles quivered, and I bit my bottom lip, turning my face up to his as desire coursed through me.

JD stared down at me, closed his eyes, and took a deep breath. Then he grasped my upper arms and tried to turn me around. "You need sleep."

I doubled my effort, shaking off his hands. "I know what I need." My hands moved up his chest, enjoying the feel of his taut muscles beneath them, and wrapped around his neck. "Don't you find me attractive?"

JD sighed and removed my arms from his neck. He held both hands and stared into my eyes. "That isn't the issue, Callie. You aren't yourself right now; you've had too much to drink."

A seed of anger flared inside, and I yanked my hands from his. "I'm fine." The feeling of rejection was sinking in yet again, "You can leave now."

"Callie – "

"No, really," I crossed my arms, "You can go."

JD shrugged and sighed. "I'll be around if you need me."

"I won't need you." With the little sobriety I had mustered, I slammed the door behind him and threw myself down on the bed. "Why? Why is this happening to me?" I thrashed back and forth and pounded my fists on the bed. "I want my perfect life back and my Daniel back," I shouted to the room. I don't know who I expected to answer me; I just needed to get the words out. Grabbing a pillow, I covered my face and screamed into it. Slowly, the screams subsided to moans, and I removed the pillow, cradling it to my chest. "I don't even care about the affair. Just send Daniel back to me please. I want my old life back." I curled into a ball as the ocean of tears poured down my cheeks until I fell into a fitful sleep.

**

JD leaned against the hallway outside Callie's room and rubbed his temples. The urge to knock on her door and talk things through coursed through his body. He hated leaving angry words as the last words. He'd promised himself after Alexa that he'd never do that again.

The more important question was why did he care so much about her? He barely knew her, but there was something in her eyes that affected him. He wanted to ease her pain and make sure she never felt any again, but what if he never saw her after this? What if he had ruined his chance with her? He couldn't remember the last time he had been so affected by a woman. His hands shook as he ran his fingers through his hair. There was nothing more he could do tonight, so he pushed himself off the wall and forced his body down the hall to his room.

When his own hotel room door closed behind him, JD crossed to the nightstand where his Bible lay. He turned to the book of John in the New Testament, where he had been reading yesterday, but the words kept swimming together. His heart still drummed too fast in his chest, so he closed the Bible and got down on his knees. Placing his elbows on the bed, he folded his hands together and leaned his forehead against them.

Blackness filled his vision but words formed in his mind and flowed out from his lips: "Lord, I don't know Callie or what her pain is about, but I sense that her heart is hurting. I want to be a good example for you before her. Please help me find the words I need to say and help me be the witness you would have me be." He remained silent, listening for the still, small voice and hoping that tomorrow he'd get a chance to see Callie again.

CHAPTER 4

he ringing of my cell phone jolted me from sleep the next morning. Eyes still closed, I patted the bed until I found my purse and pawed through it until my fingers touched the phone. Pulling it out, I swiped the screen without looking at the caller ID. "Hello?" My voice still held the heaviness of sleep.

"Callie?" My eyes snapped open at the familiar voice on the other end, and I scrambled into a sitting position, instantly awake. "Callie? Don't hang up," Daniel's voice pleaded.

My heart thudded in my chest and my pulse quickened. Why was he calling? Had he broken it off with Shaina? My nostrils flared, and my grip tightened on the phone. "Why shouldn't I?"

"I . . . okay, you have a right to, but Callie, I think I made a mistake."

"You think?" My shrill voice echoed in the hotel room, and my hands began to shake. Heat flared inside me as my eyes narrowed to slits. "You bet you did."

"I know. I know," Daniel stammered. "I just...I guess I

got cold feet, but Callie, I miss you. I can't concentrate or eat."

A small segment of satisfaction flooded me at his admission. I was glad he was suffering, now he knew how I felt. "What about Shaina?" The poison in my voice matched the ice flowing through my veins.

He sighed, "That was a one-time thing, Callie. I never meant for it to happen, but you were always so busy."

"I was trying... to get a promotion... to junior partner... to make a better life for us," I spat, biting off the string of obscenities I wanted to scream at him.

"I know and I should have been more understanding," he paused, "Hey, did you get the partnership?"

"No," I snapped. "I couldn't concentrate either, and I made some stupid mistakes. I'm lucky my boss didn't fire me."

"I'm sorry. I should have handled the situation better."

"You think?" A pregnant pause ensued, and I held the phone out, my finger hovering over the "end call" button, I should just hang up on his sorry butt, but the memory of my late-night plea made me pause. Maybe he was sorry. He did sound remorseful, but could I trust him? Would I ever be able to trust him again? I returned the phone to my ear and plucked at some lint on the comforter, waiting to hear if he had more to say.

"Can I come see you?" he blurted out.

I sucked in my breath? Did I want him here? Yes, I missed him, and I had asked for his return, but did I really want it or had that been the alcohol and JD's rejection talking? "I...I'm not home. My boss told me to take some time off, so I changed our honeymoon tickets for a trip to the Caribbean."

More silence. "Then I'll come there."

"What?" My head shot up.

"I could use some time away too, and it's not like I can't afford it. Besides I think the time together would help us reconnect."

I chewed on my thumbnail as I thought about it. The biggest question was whether I could forgive Daniel or not. Maybe it had been a one- time thing; I had been working a lot of hours, but that didn't make what he did right. Plus, we had been together for three years; that was a long time to throw away, but could I take him back? And what would my friends and family say? I sighed; I knew exactly what they would say. They would tell me to kick the creep to the curb, but they weren't the ones in love with him. If she were going to give this a try, this would be the perfect place to take the first step, away from prying eyes and accusing or pity-filled stares of those who knew. "Okay, but you'll have to get your own room."

Daniel chuckled on the other end. "Okay, it's a deal; I'll be there in a few days."

As I hung up the phone, I wondered if I had just made a horrible mistake. I wasn't the type to give cheaters a second chance, but what if there was a God who had listened and heard my plea last night, drunk though it was? *What am I saying?* Rolling my eyes, I tossed the phone down. I didn't believe in God any more than I believed in the Lochness Monster or Big Foot. *I need to clear my head. I must be suffering from extreme hunger.*

I headed down to one of the hotel restaurants on the ground floor and chose a table near a window that faced the ocean. The waiter took my order of oatmeal and fruit and then left me with my view of the enormous ocean and the waves that ebbed forward and backward – endlessly lapping the sand and then returning. The water appeared peaceful today, like a shimmering sea of blue glass. I wished my mood matched the serene picture, but churning inside me was a ball of turmoil, partly from Daniel's phone call and partly from the previous night with JD. I had no idea why, but I didn't want that to be the last impression he had of me. *Maybe I'll take a walk outside; the fresh air would do me good.* When breakfast was finished, I placed a small tip on the table and wandered out the side door to the beach.

The warmth hit me first, and my face turned up to grant the sun's kisses. The hotel had been cooler, and the warm air pressing down on my body sent a shiver down my spine. I inhaled a deep breath of the still, salty air, invigorating my senses as I strolled to the water's edge. Slipping off my shoes, I dug my toes in the sand, enjoying the feel of the tepid water licking my ankles and tickling my toes. If only I could stay here where life seemed easier and clearer.

As I turned to the right, my heart sped up at the sight of the familiar figure. The strong shoulders and longer hair gave away JD's identity before he even turned around. I opened my mouth to call to him and then shut it again. Would he want to talk to me? I had been so awful last night, but at least this would give me a chance to apologize to him. I scooped up my shoes and jogged toward him.

"JD," I hollered when I was within ear shot. He turned, and his face brightened. Relief flooded through me; he didn't seem angry.

"Hello Callie." He smiled as I stopped in front of him, "Are you feeling better this morning?"

My gaze dropped to the ground, and I dug a toe in the sand. "I am so sorry about last night. That wasn't me."

He placed a finger under my chin, lifting it until my eyes met his. Up close, his emerald green gaze was even more arresting. I felt like he was staring deep into my soul. "I know it was the alcohol talking, but Callie, maybe you should stop drinking."

My chin tingled at his touch, and I licked my lips. The

tingle was crawling down the rest of my body, which wanted to press against his. "Says the bartender who gave me a double my first night here." I had meant it as a joke, to lighten the desire I was feeling and to keep my arms from wrapping themselves around his neck, but his gaze remained serious. I cleared my throat. "The funny thing is that I rarely drink at all. This has just been a horrible week for me." His eyes never wavered from mine. How different he was from Owen who couldn't seem to keep his eyes focused on mine. The urge to lean forward and taste his lips blared in my brain, but I pushed it back.

"I was doing my job," he said finally, dropping his hand, "but your day must be getting better. You're smiling."

"Well, it might be." I tucked a dark strand of hair behind my ear and lowered my eyes. "My fiancé is coming to spend some time with me." I glanced up to see his reaction, unsure exactly why I cared.

JD's eyes widened, and his mouth parted. "Your fiancé? You mean the one who left you at the altar?"

"Well, yes," I stumbled, my toe twisting in the sand again, "but he called this morning and apologized, and maybe we can work things out." *What am I doing? He doesn't even know me and he's not convinced. Why did I say yes to Daniel?*

JD tipped his head to the side as he stared at me. "For your sake, I hope so, but I also hope you know what you are doing. Remember, Callie, sometimes things happen for a reason."

"Are you trying to tell me God planned for him to leave me?" I replied, taking a step back and lowering my brow. "Maybe Daniel's call was an indication that God wants us back together. I mean, I did pray for it."

"You prayed?" His eyebrows shot up, and his eyes gleamed.

I bit my lip. It hadn't exactly been a prayer. "Well, sort of. I asked out loud for certain things to happen."

JD's shoulders fell. "That sort of request isn't what God wants to hear from any of humanity. He wants to hear our plea for help and that we need Him to guide our lives. Besides, God isn't the only being who listens to the verbal requests and prayers we make."

"What do you mean?"

"I mean Satan also listens to what people say out loud, and he intends to interfere with God's plan for individuals – especially believers. That is the whole point of the book of Job in the Old Testament. If you haven't read it, you should."

My eyes narrowed, and I crossed my arms. Who did this guy think he was? Why couldn't he be happy for me, and why did I care so much what he thought? "Are you suggesting that my fiancé is only returning to me because Satan wants to hurt me?"

He held his palms out like a peace offering, "That's not what I said; I'm saying that Daniel's coming back to you might be Satan's doing to distract you from God's purpose for your life."

Uncrossing my arms, I moved them to my hips in a show of defiance. "Well, then why doesn't God stop it?"

JD cocked his head and gazed evenly at me. "You haven't asked him to, Callie. If you want God to influence your life, then you have to let him into your life. Jesus said that he will give us rest and carry our burdens, but we have to ask him to. We have to confess that he is Lord and that God raised him from the dead in order to be saved. Salvation is the starting point in having a working relationship with God."

I had no idea what to say to that. *Why does he have to bring God into everything?* The silence stretched out.

"Look, I head back to the states in a few days, Callie, but

I'd like to show you more of what the island has to offer while I'm here, if you're up for it."

I paused for a moment. I was a little miffed that he couldn't just be happy for me, and I certainly didn't buy into his religious nonsense, but I did have some time to kill, and he had saved me last night. Plus, as much as I wanted to, I couldn't deny that I wanted to see him again. "Sure, I'd like that."

He smiled, "Great, I want to show you Dunn's River Falls. Why don't you change into an outfit you can hike in and meet me back at the hotel entrance in half an hour?"

We walked back to the hotel, parting at the front desk to go to our separate rooms. I changed into a pair of shorts and a crop top and then made my way back to the atrium to meet JD, who stood by the front door, looking quite handsome in tan cargo shorts and a green tropical shirt.

I pointed to the bag at his feet, "Did I need to bring a bag?"

"No, I packed us a lunch, some water, and my camera. Follow me." He led the way out the front door where a grey shuttle van was waiting. As he opened the door, I noticed five other people already squished inside, and my heart sped up. Only two spots remained in the far back, just enough room for JD and myself. The space was tight, and as he scrunched in, his skin pressed against mine from the top of my shoulder down to my foot. A tingling shot down my skin, and I breathed in his clean, masculine scent.

As the van pulled out of the parking lot, I sneaked a glance at him from the corner of my eye, but his gaze focused out the window at the scenery. I took the opportunity to study his features. While his face wasn't as chiseled as Daniel's, his strong jaw commanded attention, and his soft lips eluded gentleness. What would it be like to kiss them? Would they be soft and gentle or hard and passionate? *What are you doing? You can't fall for this guy; you agreed to give Daniel a second chance.* I forced my eyes from his face and stared down at my hands. What was happening to me? My whole life, I had always been so sure of what I wanted, and now I seemed to have no clue.

A few minutes later, the van parked and everyone tumbled out. Though not extremely loud, I could hear the roar of the falls. *We must be close.* A sign near the parking indicated the direction to follow, and I fell in step beside JD as we climbed the path. "Have you been here before?"

"Yes, it's one of my favorite places, though it's much more fun to come with someone who hasn't seen it before."

His smile warmed my heart and caused another flush to spread across my face. The way he looked at me was so different from the way any other man ever had. I couldn't quite place the difference, but it made me feel special.

Trees and other green fauna surrounded us on either side as we continued up the gradual incline of the trail. My breath grew more ragged as the ascent grew steeper. I had thought I was in shape – I made it to the gym on average four times a week and walked the other days, but the incline was testing my endurance. Sweat broke out on my forehead and trickled into my eye. As I raised a hand to wipe it away, I bumped into JD's unmoving back.

"Why'd you stop?"

JD stepped to the side, and I gasped. The falls lay ahead. Clear blue water rushed over the edge, and white rocks peeked out from under the overflowing waves. The green of the jungle around complemented the blue and white foam making the view pristine and untouched. Breathless, I whispered, "Wow, it's beautiful."

He smiled and pointed to a large tree stump, "Come on, we can sit there and eat."

At the stump, he dropped his bag, and I sat down,

enjoying the opportunity to catch my breath. He pulled out two turkey sandwiches, some fruit, and some extra bread from the backpack and laid them in the middle.

I grabbed a sandwich, unwrapping the saran wrap surrounding it. "Mmm, I am so hungry." I had the fresh bread in my mouth ready to bite down when I realized JD had his face lowered and his eyes closed. *Oh, good grief.* A sigh escaped my lips, but I lowered the sandwich and closed my eyes. "Okay, fine. Go ahead and pray."

"Lord, thank you for the beauty all around us. Thank you for making yourself known in the amazing things you have created. Help us to always keep our focus on you, Amen."

My eyes snapped open at the ending word, and I took a bite of the sandwich. *This is nice. I can't remember the last time Daniel and I did anything outside.* I cocked my head, thinking back over the last few years for a time we had gone hiking or camping or even on a picnic, but came up empty. Daniel and I both worked too hard to sit down and admire nature, and when we did go out, it was almost always to fancy restaurants or less-than-memorable parties, never outside enjoying nature.

My eyes turned to JD, who was chewing his own sandwich. Suddenly I was curious about him, the rest of him that I hadn't seen yet. Did he eat like this back in the states? Did he take his dates on picnics or romantic carriage rides?

"Where do you live?" The words escaped my mouth before I could stop them, and while he raised his eyebrow at the suddenness of the question, he didn't seem put off by it.

"New York."

"Do you like it there?" I couldn't reconcile my image of busy New York with this laid back man. Did he wear a suit to work every day or jeans and a button-down shirt? Did he take the subway or walk?

"Some days," he smiled, "Sometimes it's too busy for me, and I wish I lived somewhere a little slower and less intense, but right now that's where my business is, so that's where I am. Come on," he offered a hand to help me up and then pulled a camera out of his bag. "Stand over there." He pointed to a spot where the falls would be visible to my right and a crop of beautiful rocks would fill the background.

I followed his direction, feeling self-conscious as he raised the camera, pointed it at me, and clicked the button a few times. However, the more the camera clicked, the more relaxed I became.

"My turn," I said, reaching for the camera when he paused.

"I've got a better idea." He glanced around for a minute; then he placed the camera on a tall rock. He checked the view, hit a few buttons, and ran to my side. Leaning his face in close, he whispered, "Smile."

I would have smiled anyway. There was something about him that kept a smile on my face almost constantly, but I heeded his instruction, fighting the urge to turn and look at him. The camera's audible click reached our ears, and JD collected it.

I was hoping he would take another, so I would have a reason to be close enough to breathe him in, but he packed the camera and the leftover food and threw the pack over his shoulder. We spent the rest of the afternoon hiking around the falls, taking pictures, and admiring the view. As the sun set, we made our way back to the van.

Disappointment filled me as I opened the van door. I had been looking forward to another ride with JD pressed up against me, but some of the other people must have taken an earlier shuttle because only two people filled the backseat. Sighing, I climbed into the front bench seat. JD climbed in beside me, but without another person in the seat, plenty of room still separated us.

As the van pulled up to the hotel, I dared a glance at JD. His brown hair was tousled from the hike and the wind, and my fingers itched to touch it. Would it be as soft as it looked? What would it feel like between my fingers? I wondered if he found me as attractive as I found him.

He climbed out the van first when it parked and offered a hand to help me down. My pulse skipped as heat from his hand radiated up my arm, but as soon as my feet touched the pavement he let go. Why wouldn't he hold my hand? Was it because of Daniel? Why had I told him about Daniel?

I rubbed my arm and stared into his eyes. "Thank you; today was fun and so beautiful."

His gaze locked on mine and electricity crackled between us. Could he feel it too? "You're welcome. I have to cover a shift tomorrow evening at the bar, but would you like to do lunch?"

"I'd love that." My lips parted, and I raised my chin – my sign that I wanted him to kiss me. *Come on, kiss me.* I willed the words at him and his eyes dropped to my lips. My eyes closed waiting for the feel of his lips on mine, but nothing came.

JD cleared his throat, and my eyes snapped open. "Okay, well I think I'll call it a day." He brought his hand up in an awkward wave and lumbered off to his room.

I sighed and ran my hand over my face as I watched him walk away. When I was sure he wouldn't change his mind and come sweep me up in a kiss, I returned to my own room. As I changed into pajamas, brushed my teeth, and climbed in bed, I couldn't help replaying the day in my head, though in my imagination, it always ended with a kiss.

. . .

*T*he sunlight woke me again the next morning, and as I yawned and stretched, I realized I could get used to this not waking up to an alarm clock life. I folded my arms behind my head and stared at the exposed wood ceiling wondering what JD would have in store for today. A flurry of excitement fluttered in my stomach at the mere mention of his name and I stretched out my left arm out to glance at my watch. 9:05; plenty of time to eat breakfast and soak up some sun before meeting JD.

I pulled on my swimsuit and a cover up, grabbed an apple and a bagel from the breakfast bar, and continued to the crystal blue pool. A few other people lay in chairs, either reading or listening to music. *Why didn't I think to bring a book? It would have been a perfect time to read.* Choosing a chair near a table, I peeled off my cover-up and donned my sunglasses. I had just closed my eyes when a shadow blocked the sun from my face.

"Hey beautiful," Owen leered down at me. I rolled my eyes and bit my lip to keep myself from telling him to get lost.

"I wanted to apologize about the other night and see if you wanted to get some lunch today."

Fat chance, buddy. "I already have plans for lunch, sorry." *Now please go away.*

"Dinner, then?" He was clearly not taking the hint.

"I don't think so, but thanks for asking." I closed my eyes, signaling the end of the conversation, and his shadow moved away. I let out a deep breath and continued soaking up the sun's gentle touch.

A splash in the pool and the quiet buzz of conversation told me more people had arrived, but I didn't open my eyes to see how many. I hoped no one else would bother me, but a shadow appeared above me again, and I sighed. "Owen, I said no." My eyelids flicked open and I gasped. JD, and not Owen, towered above me.

"Good thing I'm not Owen then, huh?" JD's smile was mischievous. "Are you hungry yet? I have a great place I want to show you."

I lowered my glasses and cocked an eyebrow. "I'm not dressed for a restaurant," I said, pointing to my swimwear.

"You're dressed fine for where we're going," he said.

I sat up, pulled my coverup back on, and followed him. *Where on earth could we be going that a swimsuit is appropriate attire?*

He led us out of the pool and down a quiet street into a residential neighborhood. Small peach-colored houses lined both sides of the street. An old man on his front porch lifted his hand in a wave.

I returned the wave with a lopsided, self-conscious smile. "Where are we going?"

He held up a hand, "Wait." Just past the last house on the left side, a little shop sat nestled between the houses. Three tables filled the outside area, and a barbecue pit off to one side smoldered. Tree trunks cut in half circled the tables and served as other places to sit. "This is the best barbecue in town," JD led the way to one of the tables and pulled out a chair.

"Then where is everyone?" The other two tables hosted no one, and the slight rustling of the tree leaves was the only sound.

"We're early for a reason. Wait and see."

A dark-skinned woman with long dreads and a bright green dress approached the table. "Welcome JD, you having the usual today?"

"Yes, make it two please."

The woman nodded and turned back to the small store front. She hollered something in her language, unintelligible to me, and a male voice hollered back. Soon tantalizing smells began wafting to my nose, and people began to arrive. Within minutes, the other two tables filled, and more people arrived with chairs, seemingly out of nowhere. A dozen people now dotted the little yard, and conversation hummed around us.

The woman returned with two steaming plates of barbecue, rice, and beans. This time, my fork remained untouched as I waited patiently while JD prayed before taking a bite of the delicious food. At the first bite, flavors exploded in my mouth. Typical barbecue flavors, but something else as well. Closing my eyes, I rolled the food back and forth on my tongue, trying to figure out the mysterious taste causing my taste buds to dance, but it remained elusive. When I opened my eyes again, JD was starting at me. A blush colored my cheeks, and my eyes dropped to the plate.

"How do you know of all these places?" I glanced up at JD through lowered lids.

He smiled. "I told you I come here every year, and I try something new every time I do. The good stuff I come back to every year."

"I could get used to coming here every year." A small sigh escaped my lips as I picture JD and myself having every lunch and dinner together in this tropical paradise before retiring to bed. I imagined that he would be the type of guy who wanted my head on his chest, so he could wrap his around me while I slept. Desire coursed through me again, and I felt the first fingers of heat clawing up my face. A small beeping interrupted my daydream.

JD frowned as he touched his watch. "Drat, I have to get back and get ready for work tonight."

I smiled and bit back a laugh. *Did he say "drat?" Who says "drat" anymore?*

"I'll bring some travel books over tomorrow, and we can pick another place to go," JD finished.

"That sounds great," I replied and, after paying for lunch, we traipsed back to the hotel.

As JD headed one way, I meandered to the pool to finish sunning. My previous chair was still open, so I slipped off my coverup and reclined again, thinking back to lunch. I stifled another laugh at JD's anachronistic word and lack of cursing. When was the last time Daniel had chosen a different word when he was upset? For that matter, when was the last time I had? JD might be a religious nut, but he was also positive and optimistic, which I found refreshing. Perhaps that was what made him so enjoyable to be around.

❦

*H*umming, I finished dressing and stood in front of the mirror applying makeup. My twinkling green eyes glistened back at me. I couldn't believe they were twinkling again. Just a few days with JD and the vacant stare was gone. I finished the lipstick and practiced a pout. Perhaps today would be the day he would kiss me.

A knock at my door sped my heart into overdrive, and my toes curled in excitement. *Right on time.* I skipped to the door, throwing it open, and beamed from ear to ear. "Come..." My heart stopped, and I stumbled back, covering my mouth with my hand. Instead of JD's long hair and muscular frame, Daniel's lean frame with close-cropped dark hair and blue eyes leaned in the doorway.

"Hey baby." His eyes traveled the length of my body as his arms reached for me.

I took another step back and gulped, "Daniel, hi, I, uh, wasn't expecting you so soon."

His smile faltered a little. "Well, that's not quite the greeting I was expecting. I took a red eye the night we hung up so I could get here right away. I couldn't wait to reconnect."

I blinked and tried to recover. "I'm sorry; I thought you were going to call first, but come on in." Grabbing his hand, I pulled him inside and then poked my head out and glanced down the hallway. No sign of JD yet. Sighing with relief, I closed the door and turned to Daniel. *What's he doing here so soon? He's going to ruin everything.*

He wrapped his hands around my waist and pulled me close. "How about a proper greeting?" His lips nuzzled my ear and began trailing down my neck. Pushing against his chest, I tried to extricate myself enough to keep from being in an awkward position when JD arrived. Daniel, not taking the hint, propelled me towards the bed. I stumbled, falling closer to him and breathing in his familiar scent. My resolve started to crumble and my arms found their familiar space around his neck, but a second knock jolted my head back.

"Oh," I gasped, pushing away in surprise. "That's my friend."

A flash of irritation distorted his features momentarily, but then his game face was back in place. He couldn't keep the annoyance out of his voice though. "Well, let's meet her."

I bet my lip and looked away. "Um, him," I mumbled. *Oh no, what am I going to say to JD, now?*

My heart caught in my throat as I opened the door. JD stood smiling on the other side. "Good morning friend; I brought the books." He held up a bag loaded with books.

I swallowed the lump forming in my throat. "Hi JD, come in. There's someone here I'd like you to meet."

Questions surfaced in JDs eyes, but he stepped inside; His smile froze at the sight of Daniel, and his eyes darted to me. Before I could stay anything, he painted a polite smile on his face and stepped forward with an outstretched hand. "Hello, you must be Daniel."

Daniel's eyes hardened to narrowed slits. His voice held the veiled threat of retaliation if JD didn't answer just right. "I am; and you are?"

"This is my friend JD," I said, jumping in. "He's been showing me around the island."

"Oh, well, thanks for taking care of my girl until I got here." Daniel stopped the handshake and put a possessive arm around my shoulders, pulling me close to him in a clear show of ownership. I glared up at him.

"It was my pleasure," JD replied, shifting his weight from one food to the other. "Well, um... I'm heading out, but I wanted to say good-bye and bring you these." I'd never seen JD look so uncomfortable, and I wished I had words to make it less tense.

JD put down the bag he was carrying and rifled through it a bit. He paused, seeming to consider something, and then came up with a few books and brochures. "I also found some books on the island's history you might like and some maps and brochures of the best spots to consider for exploring." He held the books out to me.

"Thank you." I ducked out of Daniel's grasp, grabbed the stack, and placed them on the dresser. The silence grew deafening as I glanced from one man to the other. *Someone say something.* JD and Daniel continued to stare at each other, like a pair of lions about to fight for the title of king. The palpable tension pressed in on me.

JD broke eye contact first. "Well, you guys have fun with what's left of your trip. It was great to meet you." His green eyes caught my gaze; unsaid words glistening in them. "Both of you." And then JD picked up his bag and left.

The door shut, and Daniel grabbed my arm, pulling me

back to him. "Well, that was awkward," he leaned in to kiss my neck again, "Now, where were we?"

I pried his hand off my arm, "Hold on a minute, Daniel." Opening the door, I ran into the hallway after JD. "I'm sorry. I . . . I didn't know he was coming today."

JD paused and then turned around. His flat voice pierced my heart. "It's okay, Callie; I have to get back to the states soon anyway." He turned to leave.

"Wait." He turned back around, silent, as if waiting for an explanation. "I... I didn't want to leave it like this," I stammered, my heart pounding in my chest.

"Callie, you have a fiancé waiting for you," his shoulders dropped, "You should get back to him." Then JD turned and walked out of my life.

I stood rooted in the hallway, watching him leave. A tightness in in stomach emerged, doubling me over. What had I done? Would I ever see him again? Why did I care so much? Leaning my head back, I took a few deep breaths, before standing and trudging back to the room.

Daniel's rigid posture and folded arms greeted me when I crossed the threshold. "What was that about? Were you seeing him?"

I tensed at the biting tone in his voice. "It wasn't like that." Suddenly, a spark of anger flared inside me, and I took a bold step, jabbing my finger at him. "Besides who are you to question me? I'm still not sure I have forgiven you. You did sleep with my best friend and leave me, through a text of all things, on our wedding day."

He raised his left hand to ward off my angry advance. "Alright, you're right, but geeze Callie, it was one time, and I said I was sorry."

"I know you're sorry, but it isn't easy to forget an experience like that." My throat closed up, and I swallowed back tears.

Daniel's body relaxed as he took a step forward, "I understand, but I promise I will spend my life making it up to you."

I stared at him a moment longer; questions raging in my mind. Could he really change, or was this all an act? Could I care for him again? Daniel's blue eyes pleaded with me, and the wall of resolve chipped away. I took a step and let him wrap his arms around me, but I couldn't stop the thought that I was staying with the wrong man.

CHAPTER 5

*T*hough not in the same way as JD, Daniel had been very attentive and enjoyable the final two weeks spent in the Caribbean. That no one knew who we were or what our past entailed had calmed my nerves, and I was almost able to imagine the time together was like a honeymoon.

However, as we headed back to my apartment in Mesquite, my unease grew. What would my friends say? What would my mother say? JD's reaction had been utter shock, and he had barely known me; how much worse would the reaction be of those who did?

Daniel squeezed my knee, "You're quiet."

"Hmm?" I removed the thumbnail I had been chewing from my mouth. "I'm sorry; I was thinking about what to tell people regarding what happened between us."

"Who cares what they say?" A note of agitation crept in his voice.

I scrunched down in my seat at his forceful tone. "That's easy for you to say, but you weren't the one cheated on and left alone at the altar."

His hands tightened on the steering wheel, and his jaw clenched. The vein in the side of his neck pulsed out. "How long am I going to have to keep apologizing?"

"I don't know," I said, my own anger building, "but try to see it from my side. If I had cheated, left you, and then come back, what would your friends say?"

Daniel relaxed his hands and flashed his charming smile. "They'd say I was lucky because you are so beautiful."

He knew I was a sucker for his smile, but I wasn't buying what he was selling today. *Quit trying to change the subject.* "I'm serious."

"Okay, okay, you're right. If you think it will help, I will apologize to any of your friends and family personally, okay?"

I nodded, but the pit of uneasiness extended its tendrils up to my heart cutting right through Daniel's flippant words.

As my apartment came into view, my heart lightened. It had been nice having some time away, but I was looking forward to the familiar. I carried my bag into the bedroom and began to unpack. Under all the clothes, at the bottom of the bag, the books from JD lay. I picked the top one up, opening the cover, but before I could read anything, Daniel entered the room and wrapped his arms around me. The book fell from my hand as he pulled me backward onto the deep purple bedspread.

"Ah, I've missed being in this bed with you. What do you say we refresh my memory of how much I enjoyed this?" He pulled me close, meeting my lips. Familiarity took over, and my body melted into his as his lips roamed down my neck.

A few hours later, I awoke with a start. Something wasn't right. I lay still for a minute, listening; then I jumped up and raced into the bathroom, reaching the toilet as my stomach heaved its contents out. *Whoa, what was that about?* I washed my mouth out and splashed water on my face, noting the paler-than-normal complexion as I looked in the mirror. After drying my face, I headed back to bed.

"Everything okay?" Daniel words were mumbled from the bed without even opening his eyes.

Irritation flared inside me as I crawled back in beside him. "I don't know; it might have been something I ate." I spent the rest of the day in bed, in and out of consciousness.

*T*he feeling wasn't gone the next morning, but it seemed less intense as I lay in bed breathing. Deciding I was okay, I swung my legs off the bed and plodded to the closet.

Daniel came up behind me and pushed my hair to one side so his lips could have easy access to my neck. "Are you really going into work today? We just got in last night."

"I have to. I need to prove I'm still partner material, even though I'm going to have to wait a whole year to get it." I pulled my favorite black skirt off the hanger and ducked out of his reach so I could pull it on. It slipped on easily enough, but the zipper wouldn't go all the way up. "Ugh." I shimmied out of it, tossing it on the floor and reached for another skirt. It didn't fit either and neither did the third. Frustration surged through me. What was going on? Finally, an older skirt with an elastic waist slipped on.

"Eat a little too well while you were gone, did you?" Daniel asked, noticing my choice of skirts.

I wasn't sure if he were teasing or hinting that I needed to go on a diet, so I glared at him for good measure as I yanked a long blue shirt off the hanger that would cover the hideous elastic waist. It was not my usual put-together look, but it worked. "I'll be back later," I said, pushing past Daniel. "Don't make a mess while I'm gone."

Without kissing him goodbye, I left the apartment. I was miffed at his ribbing and contemplating if I already regretted letting him back in my life. JD would never have said something so insensitive. JD? Where had that thought come from? I hadn't seen him in two weeks. He was probably back in New York doing whatever he did there. Shaking my head to clear his smiling face, I focused on paying attention to traffic as I drove to the office.

Tina stood, smiling, as I neared the office. "Welcome back. How was your trip?"

"It was good.... and interesting." I thought about telling Tina I was back with Daniel, but the memory of her earlier reaction and opinion of Daniel flooded my mind. *No reason to face the disappointment in case it doesn't work out. I'll tell her in a few weeks if he's still in the picture.*

Tina raised an eyebrow, but didn't press the issue. "Okay, well the work is on your desk, in piles, and here are your messages."

As I reached for the messages, my stomach turned again. Clapping a hand over my mouth, I bolted down the hall to the bathroom, making it to the stall just in time.

When my stomach was empty and still, I gargled some water to lessen the lingering taste in my mouth and splashed some water on my face. The color of my face was not right, and there were splotches that had never been there before. *What is wrong with me?* I gave it a few more minutes to make sure there wouldn't be a repeat performance, and then I headed back to the office.

Tina's eyes were wide. "Are you alright?"

"Yeah, it's food poisoning, I think. It started yesterday when we got back. I feel fine otherwise though. In fact, I seem to have gained weight even with my frequent deposits to the porcelain god." I meant it to sound light – joking was a habit when I got uncomfortable – but the words sounded flat even to me.

Tina wasn't buying it either. "Food poisoning doesn't usually last that long," her voice oozed concern. "Promise me you'll go to the doctor if this keeps up."

"I promise." I flicked my hand, dismissing the conversation, and headed into the office to tackle the mountain of work. It hit me as I closed the office door that I had said "we" instead of "I." Thankfully, Tina hadn't noticed, but I would have to be more careful in the future.

My food stayed down the rest of the day, and I got so engrossed in work that I forgot my promise to Tina. I climbed in my car, planning to head to the gym, but Tina's words reared their ugly head and bounced around in my head, and instead my car pulled into a local emergency clinic.

I entered the small grey clinic, and a petite brunette with glasses looked up from the desk. "Can I help you?"

"I hope so," I said, signing the check in form on the counter, "I've been vomiting several times for the last twelve hours. I figured it was food poisoning, but my friend thought I should see a doctor."

"That's probably a good idea," the receptionist agreed. "Have a seat, and we'll call you back shortly."

I sat down in one of the many empty chairs and picked up a magazine from the table next to me. On the cover, a couple on a beach lounged in chairs. It looked so much like the ocean in the Caribbean that my thoughts wandered back to that time. *I wonder what JD is doing now?* There they were again, thoughts of JD crowding into my head.

"Callie Green?" A short, stocky nurse with dark hair

stood at the open door, clipboard in hand. Her eyes scanned the waiting room.

I set the magazine down and followed her into another small grey room. A computer terminal with a stool in front of it and one other grey plastic chair were the only furniture in the room. As I assumed the stool was for the nurse, I took a seat in the chair.

"Any fever?" the nurse asked as she began taking my vitals.

I shook my head. "I don't think so; I haven't felt hot anyway."

The nurse ran the thermometer across my forehead. "98.6, that's normal. Any other aches or pains?"

"No, but I just got back from the Caribbean. Could I have picked up something there that's made me sick?"

"It's possible." The nurse sat on the stool and began typing on the computer, filling in the electronic chart. "We will look at all the possibilities. Have you had intimate relations in the last month?"

I blinked, taken aback by the prying question. "What does that have to do with anything?"

The nurse paused her typing and turned her hazel eyes on me. "It could be significant if you've also been tired lately, have you?"

I shrugged. "Maybe a little more than usual, but as I said I just got back from vacation. I think it's probably jet lag, you know?"

The nurse looked at me again, raised an eyebrow, and then turned back to the computer screen. "Okay, well the doctor will be in soon." She exited, leaving me alone in the small room.

As I glanced around the bland room, I pondered the nurse's questions. Could she be insinuating an STD? I thought back to High School health class. Was vomiting a symptom of any STD? Not like it mattered, Daniel and I always used protection anyway. He always claimed he wasn't ready for a family yet. I couldn't remember the last time we . . . and then the night with Brent flashed in my head. I sucked in a large gulp of air. What had that been, three or four weeks ago? Pulling out my phone, I furiously tapped the calendar app. *One , two, three...Oh no, I haven't had a period in six weeks.* My fingers touched my parted lips as a coldness erupted in my core.

The doctor, an older woman with greying hair but kind eyes, entered at that moment. She registered the shock on my face. "Are you alright?"

"Could I? I mean, is it possible . . . Am I pregnant?" The cold clamored through my insides sending a shiver down my spine.

A warm smile spread across the woman's face. "I was about to ask you the same question."

"We are always careful, but there was this one night...." I dropped my head as the guilt of what I had done roiled around in my stomach. It weighed on me like the heavy anchor of a large ship that had been thrown overboard.

"It only takes once," the doctor laughed. She picked up a small cylindrical container off the counter tray and handed it to me, "Here, provide me a urine sample, and we can know in ten minutes." After pointing out the bathroom down the hall, the doctor left. and I fought for air.

I brought my knees to my chest and wrapped my arms around them. *Oh no, not again. I can't be pregnant; I can't.* I was trying to make it work with Daniel; I was trying to become partner; and I was pretty sure the baby would belong to a man I had met once. Once! This wasn't me, and this definitely did not fit in my perfect plan. After a few calming breaths, I grabbed the plastic container and headed down the hall to the bathroom.

My hands were shaking as I unscrewed the lid and filled the jar. When finished, I set the cup in the cupboard that opened to a lab on the other side and washed my hands. Back to the small grey room to wait. The hallway seemed longer, like I was walking to a death sentence. My feet felt heavy and clunky, the way they feel when you try to run through mud.

I sat back down in the chair and stared at my watch, watching the second-hand turn, my mind blank. A knock at the door jolted me back to reality, and I raised my head.

"I have your results back," the doctor held a small white piece of paper in her hand. "Would you like to read them, or shall I give them to you orally?"

"Um, I'll read them, I guess." I swallowed hard and reached for the folded white paper.

"Here you go. Take your time, and I'll be back in a few minutes to answer any questions you might have."

I stared at the paper burning into my hand. The words on this paper could change my life. Icy fear returned, clawing up my neck. I took a deep breath and unfolded the paper. My eyes scanned it but no words registered until the all caps "PREGNANT." It mocked me with its capital letters. What was I going to do?

The doctor reappeared a few minutes later. "Have you had time to look over the paper?"

I nodded, unable to form words.

"I can tell this is a bit of a shock for you, but I don't think there's anything else wrong with you. Do you want information on options?"

"Options?" I asked in a haze, the words fuzzy in my mouth.

"You know, what to do about your pregnancy. My dear, you can keep it, put it up for adoption, or have an abortion. I can give you great names to consider for all three choices, if you want them," the doctor gathered some pamphlets from the clear plastic holder on the wall as she spoke.

Grey fog surrounded me, making my voice sound distant, "Okay, I guess I should take all three."

"It's still early in your pregnancy, so you have time to think about what to do, but if you choose abortion, you shouldn't wait too much longer." The doctor pulled a business card from her pocket and wrote names and numbers down on the back of it. "The first one is for a counselor if you decide to keep the baby and need help while carrying it. The second one is of a local adoption agency, and the third is an abortion clinic that is down on State Street. And here are some pamphlets to read about pregnancy."

I took the paperwork and stared at the white card, my mind still foggy. In a daze, I gathered up my things and left the room, moving on autopilot. I stopped only once, at the receptionist's desk to pay for the services, before leaving the building.

When I got to the parking lot, I opened my driver's side door, sat down, and shut the door. I put the key in the ignition but didn't turn it on. My hands shook on the steering wheel, and I stared out the windshield at nothing. What was I going to do?

Daniel had always stated he didn't want a family right away and I had agreed, because kids before age thirty had not been in my perfect plan, but was I sure Daniel and I would last? If we didn't, could I raise a child alone? I supposed I could put the baby up for adoption, but that would mean going through all the pain of pregnancy and gaining all that weight to give the baby to someone else in the end. I didn't know if I could do that. That left abortion. Though I'd always been "pro-choice" in general, I had never thought I'd have to make the choice myself. It couldn't hurt to at least look into it. I stared down at the card and found my fingers punching the number in my phone.

"State Street Clinic," the lady on the other end of the phone said after the second ring.

I jumped at the voice, though I didn't know why. Had I been expecting a machine? "Uh hi, I was hoping to get your address, so I could swing by and ask some questions."

"1400 State Street, and we are open till 7 P.M."

Fifteen minutes later, I pulled into the parking lot and stared at the small brick building. Was this really what I wanted to do? I exited the car and glanced around for a sign, but none hung on the building. I started up the small cement path, dotted only by a few trees and finally saw a small stenciling on the door that told me I was in the right place.

Just before the entrance, an older black woman sat in a wheelchair next to a green bench. She held a sign in her hands that read: Abortion stops a beating heart. I stared at her, and the woman returned the gaze. Then, she bowed her head. *Oh, no, not more prayers.* I hurried past the woman and opened the door.

The room was small, but comfortable looking with a few chairs and a TV on the wall. Two young girls looked up as I entered, fear evident in their eyes. A petite brunette with glasses and a messy bun sat at the desk answering the phones and typing on a keyboard. She finished the current call and glanced up at me.

"Can I help you?"

I rubbed the business card in my hand. "Maybe; I was given this number by a doctor to talk to someone about having an abortion."

"Have you decided to schedule one?" The lady tapped the mouse a few times to open a date book.

"Um, not yet. I don't really know much about them and

was hoping you had some information I could read, to better understand the process."

"Sure, there are pamphlets over there you can take," she pointed to her left and returned to her computer, dismissing me at the same time.

I crossed to the wooden rack hanging on the wall, picked up a pamphlet, and sat down to read it. The pamphlet explained how the "lump of cells" would be suctioned out. I bit my lip and cocked my head to the side. *Lump of cells, is that all it is right now? And if so when does it become a baby?*

Returning to the desk, I tapped the counter to get the woman's attention, "Um, excuse me."

"Yes?" The woman didn't look up, just kept clicking on her computer keys.

"Does it hurt?"

"You might be sore for a few days, but it's not that bad."

I shook my head. "No, I meant does it hurt the baby? I mean will the baby feel pain?"

The woman stopped typing and turned a blank face to me. "It's not a baby. It's a lump of cells."

"So, when does it become a baby?"

The woman took a deep breath and then sighed. "When it's born; do you want to schedule?"

I didn't feel like I was asking dumb questions, but the abrupt response of the woman made me uncertain. "Um, I don't know yet. How soon do I have to decide?"

The woman pushed her glasses up her nose. "It's best to have it done before 12 weeks, but you can do it as late as 24 weeks, although if you wait that long the process costs a little more."

"Why?"

"Why what?" Irritation laced the woman's voice. She obviously did not enjoy all of my questions, which I found confusing. Weren't these people supposed to help me decide?

"Why does it cost more?" I repeated.

The woman dropped her head and picked at something unseen on her pants. "There's more to remove because the cells are bigger then."

I raised an eyebrow at her. What wasn't she saying? "Okay, thank you." The woman turned back to her computer and resumed her tapping.

I tucked the brochure in my purse to read it more thoroughly later. My analytical mind had begun to whir, and it wouldn't allow accept such hollow answers without research. I was glad Daniel had texted that he was working tonight because I didn't think I would be able to hide this secret from him for long and I wasn't quite ready to tell him about it yet.

"God has a purpose for your baby." The words pulled at my heart, and I stopped.

"Excuse me?" I asked, whirling to face the woman.

"I can see the pain in your face, but death is not the answer. This baby was made by God, and He has a plan for it."

Anger sparked within me. "Yeah, well it's my body, so I can do what I want with it," I snapped back and continued to my car. *Sheesh, why can't people keep their opinions to themselves?*

*O*nce home, I sat on the couch and pulled out the brochure again. The brochure portrayed the procedure as quick and easy, but questions swirled in my head. *If it isn't a baby yet, it wouldn't really be murder, would it? I mean I barely knew the father, and I doubt Daniel would stick around to support me and a baby by another man. This would be easier. I can pretend it never happened and get on with my life, and I'll never make that mistake again.* An odd sensation stirred in my stomach, but

I put the brochure away, dismissed the thought, and headed to bed.

As I pulled back the blanket, a colored corner of something on the floor caught my attention. Bending down, I picked up a travel book. It was one of the books that JD had given me the day he left; it must have fallen from my bag when I was unpacking. Giving no further thought to it, I tossed it on the bed and plodded into the bathroom for my nightly routine.

As I brushed my teeth, I turned sideways and eyed my belly in the mirror. Was it really only a lump of cells? What would it look like? Was it a boy or a girl? I shook my head to clear it. No use thinking like that if I wasn't going to keep it. I finished brushing and flossing and then climbed into bed. The travel book caught my eye again and I opened it. A picture fluttered out, and as I picked it up, I gasped. The picture of JD and I atop Dunn's Falls stared back at me.

I traced his face and then looked at my own happy smile. Turning it over, I found a note scrawled in pen:

*D*ear Callie,
I enjoyed our time together. I hope everything works out for you and your fiancé, but if it doesn't, please remember that you are loved by the God of Heaven. He loves you and is always looking out for you. If you let Him, He will bless you in abundant ways. I'm not leaving my number as it wouldn't be appropriate right now, but know that I will be thinking of you, will pray for you, and if it is in God's plan, then we will meet again. –JD

. . .

I read the note again and again as I thought back to the time spent with JD. He had been so different and so refreshing, but I wondered how he would react if he knew my latest news. He hadn't been like other men and he never seemed to want anything from me, but would he still find me attractive if he knew I was pregnant? Then reality crashed in again. Why was I even thinking about JD? Other than New York, I had no idea where he lived. I didn't even know his last name. The chances that I would ever see him again were abysmal. Sighing, I set the picture on my nightstand and turned off the light, falling into a fitful sleep.

**

JD sighed as he finished his dinner for one, yet again. It wasn't that he wanted to be alone, but after his last relationship he'd become pretty picky. The good news was that he was becoming a half decent cook. He had tried microwave dinners for a time after Alexa, but those had grown old quickly. Then he'd taken to dropping in to see his parents, right around dinner time, in the hopes of a home-cooked meal, but now they were in Florida and he was in New York, a little far to go for dinner. So, he'd taken up watching cooking shows in the evening after work and he'd learned how to make a few decent meals.

He placed his plate and utensils in the dishwasher and wiped up the counter. Walking into his living room, he sat down in his favorite blue recliner, turned on the TV, flipped through a few channels, and turned it off again. Nothing on TV appealed to him anymore. He picked up the book he had been reading from his coffee table, and his eyes landed on a piece of paper. It was his prayer list. *No time like the present.*

Scanning the list, JD sent up prayers for each name. When he finished, he placed the paper back down, but an unease in his stomach called him back. He perused it again; he had prayed for everyone on the list, but the feeling did not abate. *Did I forget someone?* He closed his eyes, trying to remember if he had forgotten to write one down, but nothing came to mind. Shrugging, he placed the list down again and froze. Images of Callie flooded his mind. He hadn't thought of her in weeks, but tonight the feeling was strong. He fell to his knees, and whispered a prayer for her.

CHAPTER 6

"*M*ommy?"

I woke up and glanced around trying to find the owner of the voice. A small girl, about the age of three, with long blond hair and blue eyes stood by my bed, little hands hanging on the edge.

"Mommy? Why didn't you want me?" Tears glistened in the girl's big blue eyes, and her lips formed into a pout.

"What do you mean?"

"Why didn't you want me? You had me in your tummy, and you let them cut me and suck me out?"

The anguish on the cherub face tugged at my heart, and my breath caught in my throat. "They cut you up? But, they told me it was a bunch of cells, not a baby yet."

"Mommy, I had a heartbeat and a brain. I felt everything they did to me. Didn't you feel me try to move away from that thing? Aren't mommies supposed to protect their children?"

"I..." I stammered, but no answer came. My forehead wrinkled; mommies were supposed to protect their children, weren't they?

The little girl's eyes dropped to look at her hands. "Was I not pretty enough? Did I make you mad?"

"Oh, honey, I wasn't mad. You are beautiful. I... I wasn't ready to have a baby, I guess, and it was my choice."

"What about my choice, mommy?"

Again my mouth opened, but no sound came out. I had never considered that question. I believed that what I did with my body was my choice alone, but here was this tiny life showing me that she too had a body and a desire to live. "I'm so sorry." The little girl was so beautiful and angelic. The child began to fade. "Where are you going?" I stretched out a hand to touch her, but the girl was too far away.

"I have to go, but mommy, I would have loved you; I really would have."

The girl faded, and I woke with tears running down my face. My eyes searched around the dark room, but there was no girl; it had all been a dream. I placed a hand on my stomach, but nothing moved yet. Could it be true?

I clamored from bed and retrieved my laptop from the desk. Taking it back to bed, I propped up some pillows and turned it on. Where to begin? I typed in "abortion procedures" and pages after pages filled the screen. The "procedure" was much more graphic than the brochure from the clinic had claimed. In fact, it seemed almost barbaric, but there was a non-medical procedure, a pill I could take if I was early enough. That seemed less awful until I read that the women were usually just sent home to have the miscarriage themselves. The thought of what I might see as I miscarried made that an unappealing option as well.

As I kept scouring, I ran across a page discussing side effects of abortions. *There are side effects?* I clicked the link and stories of women who regretted their abortions littered the page. There were stories of women having miscarriages or ectopic pregnancies after abortions and stories of women having hysterectomies in their mid-twenties because of previous abortions. Fear coiled in me like a spring. I didn't want a baby right now, but I did want one in the future. If I aborted this baby, would I have pregnancy issues later like these women? I tried to convince myself that there couldn't be that many instances of these complications because I'd never heard of any. The media certainly had never mentioned them.

I scrolled back to the top of the page and searched for abortion side effects. Again, links filled the screen. I clicked the first one, and my eyes devoured the page. Thirty percent? The spring coiled tighter. Thirty percent of women who had abortions went on to have reproductive issues including miscarriages, premature babies, and infertility? More than half of all women later suffered from mental health issues including depression and suicide. The coiled spring turned cold, and my mouth dropped open. How had the media never discussed these statistics? Wasn't it their job to give all the information? I bit the inside of my lip. Thirty percent wasn't the biggest number, but what if I wanted to have a baby in the future and couldn't?

The alarm blared beside me, causing me to jump and shut the laptop in surprise. Could it be time to get up for work already? My stomach still churned like I'd just gotten off a roller coaster, and the fear gripped ever tighter. *I'll have to tell Daniel about this and get his opinion. After all, it could affect him too.*

I wiped my palms on my skirt as I exited the car. Pulling my shoulders back to portray a confidence I didn't feel, I entered the coffee shop. Daniel stood at the counter ordering; I took a deep breath and marched up to him. As I touched his arm, he whirled to glare at me, but his eyes softened when he realized it was not some stranger.

"You're late, so I ordered for you already." Agitation colored his voice, and I cringed. This wasn't going to be easy.

I cleared my throat and swallowed a few times, "How was your morning?"

"It was awful." He grabbed a pastry and our coffees and led the way to the last empty table. A few other couples were in the small cafe, but singles with laptops comprised most of the crowd. "I had meeting after meeting that accomplished nothing. It was ridiculous . . ."

As he droned on about his frustration, I ran my finger along the coffee cup lid. I wished he didn't sound so angry, but maybe the coffee and pastry would relax him. A few nearby patrons glared at Daniel's loud voice before returning to their work. I continued listening, waiting for a softer side to emerge, but Daniel's posture never loosened. He checked his watch and rolled his eyes which I assumed meant he had to get back to work. It wasn't the perfect time, but if I didn't ask now, I might not get the chance.

"Daniel," I said, putting my hand on his arm to keep him from standing, "how would you feel about having a baby?"

He turned his mouth down and stiffened. "A baby?" The nearby heads popped up again, agitation in their eyes. His voice had not been quiet. "Did you not hear me talking about how stressful work was? A baby would make it worse. You aren't pregnant, are you?"

I bit my lip. This wasn't going as planned.

His nostrils flared and he lowered his voice to a harsh whisper, "Callie, how could you be so irresponsible?"

My teeth clenched together, "In case you forgot, it takes two people to make a baby."

He leaned back in his chair and stared at me. "I know

that, but I thought you were on the pill. You were supposed to take care of that."

His words stung, and I drew a deep breath, sending back my own biting words, "Well, I guess in the whole leaving me at the altar thing, I might have forgotten to take them for a while."

"Oh, here we go again," he threw his hands in the air. "Is that always going to be your excuse? I left you at the altar?"

My eyes narrowed, "Well, you did, and it had repercussions."

"Look," he took a deep breath and ran a hand through his dark hair, "that event is behind us; it's water under the bridge, but surely you can see that a baby would not be good right now. We have to take care of us first. Get an abortion and be done with it. Then we can move on with our lives."

I looked down at my hands. Had he always sounded so callous and selfish? "I've been doing some research on the matter though, Daniel, and I found that thirty percent of women who have abortions either have trouble conceiving later or have pregnancy complications because of it. What if I can't have a child later, when we might want one?"

Daniel waved his hand and scoffed, "Thirty percent is nothing. Think about the seventy percent that aren't affected. That is a much bigger number." The wall of defense that I had built earlier began to crumble under Daniel's harsh words.

I leaned forward, splaying my hands on the table and playing my last card. "Yes, but don't you think it's a baby? Isn't it murder then?"

"Come on, do you think the Supreme Court would honor the procedure if it were murder?" he smirked. "It's a bunch of cells right now, so think of having an abortion like removing a scab from a sore."

My face wrinkled in disgust at the thought. "Still the

procedure seemed pretty gruesome, Daniel; they cut the baby up and then suck it from the womb. I saw pictures of cut up little arms and legs online."

He flicked his hand, dismissing my concerns. "First off, those pictures are doctored; you can't believe everything you read online. Besides, you have to think about us, about yourself. Do you think you could make partner while trying to raise a baby? Then, there's the problem of our schedules – we both work long hours and would have no time for a baby. Wouldn't it be worse to raise a baby we didn't have time for?"

His words began to make sense in my mind. I didn't have time for a baby, and surely the mass in my belly was only cells right now; it was still early in the pregnancy. A small voice inside insisted again that it was wrong, but Daniel's words were louder and the fear of the unknown drowned it out. "Okay, I'll think about it again," I agreed.

He frowned, but let the subject drop.

That night I eyed the bed warily as I undressed. Though I still wasn't comfortable with the decision, I had decided the abortion did make more sense. All of Daniel's arguments were true, but the dream from the previous night continued to haunt me. I didn't want to see the girl again, my daughter? I didn't want to feel the guilt. Climbing into bed, I turned on the TV, hoping for some mindless entertainment. Though I fought sleep as long as I could, eventually my lids fell closed.

My eyes opened to a clear blue sky and a field of white daisies. A small child's hand was encased in my own. I looked down to the top of a blond head. The girl appeared younger this time, maybe eighteen months, walking but not super steady on her feet. Her blue eyes locked on mine and then filled with tears, which streamed down her face.

"What's wrong, baby girl?" I picked up the girl and brushed her hair back.

"Why you not want me? Why you let them take me from you?" The baby's face scrunched and loud sobs escaped her mouth. I searched for words of comfort, but none came. This defenseless baby girl was crying because of my selfish choice, and I could say nothing to soften the pain.

I awoke covered in sweat this time. Was it going to be like this every night? What would happen when I had the abortion? Would the girl go away then? Or would I become like the eighty percent who had emotional repercussions? Questions paraded through my mind, one after the other. I turned the TV back on and watched infomercials till morning, trying to erase the beautiful face of the baby from my dreams.

*A*s I poured my third cup of coffee that day, I fought the emotional turmoil in my stomach. I had to schedule the appointment once and for all. I couldn't keep losing sleep like I had the last two nights or I would get fired. Picking up the phone, I dialed the abortion clinic and set an appointment for later that afternoon. I had expected a feeling of peace now that the decision was made, but a feeling of dread blanketed me instead.

I pulled into the parking lot of the clinic that afternoon after work and sighed. The same older black lady, who had been there before, sat by the front door. *Oh great, just what I don't need.* Locking the car, I ducked my head and strode past the woman. *Please don't talk to me. Please don't talk to me.*

"Please don't kill your baby." The woman's pleading voice reached me just as my fingers touched the door handle.

I stopped, heat searing up my spine. I turned and faced the woman, lashing out at her. "I'm sorry, but what business is it of yours?"

The woman cocked her head and stared at me. Her dark eyes contained a deep sadness. "Can I tell you my story?" She folded her hands in her lap, "And then I'll never bother you again."

I shifted from one foot to another and bit my lip. I didn't know this woman or care to hear her story, but my stomach was curdling again and something told me to give the woman a few minutes. "Fine, go ahead."

The woman paused, closed her eyes for a second, and took a deep breath. "My name is Sandra Dobbs. When I was twenty-five, I thought I had my whole life ahead of me. I was planning to be a nurse, but I made the mistake of being intimate with my boyfriend, Peter, and found myself pregnant. I wanted that baby, but we were young; he was a med student and he didn't have time right then for fatherhood. We fought for a few weeks, but in the end, he won, and pressured me into having an abortion."

My head fell forward, and my eyes widened. It was like this lady's story was my own. My hands curled into fists as the emotions battled inside of me. One part wanted to stay and hear the story, the other wanted to flea and pretend it had never happened.

"I knew I shouldn't have been intimate outside of marriage, and though I wanted a baby, I too agreed it wasn't the right time to have one, so I went through the 'procedure.' On one hand, I was relieved, but on the other, guilt plagued me afterwards. I became withdrawn and started drinking, and Peter and I split up. My drinking grew worse, but then I met a wonderful man, Henry, and he started bringing me to church. I stopped drinking for a time and told him I thought I had accepted God, but I don't think I really had. I hoped if I acted like everyone else that He would forgive me, even though I couldn't forgive myself. My life seemed fine; Henry proposed to me; and we got married. For several months, I think I was happy, and then things changed. We couldn't get pregnant. After two years of trying, I went to a doctor to see what the issue might be. It turns out the 'procedure' had damaged my ability to ever have a baby."

I clapped my hand to my mouth. *Is she reading my mind? How could she know this is my biggest fear?* As my knees buckled, I grabbed the wall of the building to steady myself. The brick scratched against my palms, but I barely felt the pain.

"Well, my husband didn't know I'd had an abortion before we were married. In fact, I'd never told anyone but my closest friend, but I made the mistake of telling him about it on the way home from dinner that night. He was so upset in finding out that he lost control of the car and swerved into oncoming traffic, over-corrected, and sent us careening into a tree. The crash paralyzed me from my waist down and Henry suffered from a concussion and a pretty bad skull fracture. In one night, that "easy" decision I had made five years earlier produced a drastic result. It destroyed my baby and the life I wanted to have. For years now, I have wished thousands of times that I had just kept Isaac.

"You know your baby was a boy?" I shivered as ice slipped through my veins.

"I didn't at first, but then the dreams came."

My knees buckled again. "He visits you in your dreams?"

"Nearly every night." Tears shone in the woman's dark brown eyes. "At first, I hated those dreams because having an abortion was 'my choice,' and I didn't like the guilt that greeted me every morning when I woke up. Eventually though, I realized that those dreams were the only link I would ever have to the biological child I could have had. He would have been 35 this year, and sometimes in the dreams I get the sense he would have married and had two or three kids himself. Not a day goes by that I don't regret that decision I made so long ago. Now, I know what happened to me won't happen to everyone, but do you want to take the chance of experiencing that risk?"

I stumbled to the nearby bench and hung my head. My hands shook with the intense emotion flooding my body. "I don't want that to happen to me, but how do I keep this baby when my fiancé doesn't want it?"

"Do you know the Lord?" Sandra placed a warm brown hand on my shoulder.

I shook my head and sighed. "My mom does, I think, but how is that going to help me?"

"Ah child, God loves you and wouldn't want you to do anything against his will, so if your fiancé loves you, and if he is a Christian, then he shouldn't want you to do anything against God's will either. As for me, I have no doubt that abortion is against God's will. He has made us all in his image and if we destroy that image, then we are telling God He isn't important. Look... um... I'm sorry, what can I call you, dear?"

"Callie. Callie Green."

The woman blinked, and her mouth fell open. "Callie Green? Is your mother Melanie Green?"

I lifted my head to see the beginning of a smile stretching across Sandra's face. "Yes, she is; how did you know that?"

Her grin grew even bigger, her dark brown eyes sparkling. "Your mother goes to my church. She called me a few weeks ago and asked me to pray for you because your fiancé had left you. I've been praying ever since." Her face grew serious, "Is your fiancé back in the picture then?"

Heat flooded my face, and I stared down at my feet. "I'm

not sure. He apologized and I thought he meant it, but now I'm seeing a side of him I never saw before, and I'm not sure I like it. Have you really been praying for me for weeks?"

"Yes; and so have the rest of the prayer warriors I'm affiliated with. There's about fifty of us; so you see, God must have a plan for this baby, because we didn't even know you were pregnant. In fact, God led me to pray double for you as I've prayed for you since the first time I saw you here, not knowing you were already on my prayer list."I stared at Sandra, eyes wide. "Why would you pray for a complete stranger?"

Sandra sat back, but her eyes still shone. "Well, because that is what Jesus commissioned us to do. As Christians, we are to pray unceasingly, and believers in Christ are to tell as many people about him as we can." Her eyes dulled and she stared down at her hands for a minute. When she raised her head, tears sat on her lids. "But I also prayed for you due to my own past. Because of my poor choice and its consequences, this," she pointed to the clinic, "is where I pray for the girls and women who come to make the same terrible decision I did. I see this effort as ministry before my Lord."

I tilted my head and raised an eyebrow. "How do you still seem so peaceful and happy after everything you have gone through?"

Sandra smiled, but it appeared smaller than before, and her eyes clouded over. "Life isn't always easy, dear. I still have many tough days, but Jesus is my peace. I pray to Him whenever I feel sad, and He eases my pain."

I thought of JD and how very much like him Sandra sounded. "I don't think I've ever known anyone so strong with so much pain in their past."

Sandra dropped her head. "I wasn't always strong. After the accident, I hit rock bottom. I reverted back to drinking, so I could dull the pain. I almost lost my marriage to Henry, but God sent Pastor Tony to us." She smiled, and her eyes glazed as she continued, "Henry forced me to go to counseling with him, and Pastor Tony showed me how my life could still have purpose. He and his wife, Margaret, showed me real love. I mean, the love of Jesus shone through that man and his wife, and he showed me how to pray. He even gave me a leather prayer journal, and this time I really did come to know God. They arranged an interview for a job so I could get back on my feet, and they connected us with an adoption agency. If God hadn't sent those two, I don't know where I'd be, but you see with Jesus, you can do anything. And remember, if your fiancé tries to pressure you again or gives you an ultimatum, and if you lose him because you don't do what he wants, Jesus will be there for you."

"Is that true, even if I'm not a believer in Him?"

Sandra's eyes crinkled as a small laugh escaped her lips. "Yes, even then, because He died for you. Have you ever heard of John 3:16?"

I shook my head. I couldn't remember the last time I had read anything in a Bible, though I was almost certain I had one somewhere at home, a present from my mother one Christmas. I hadn't bothered to read it, and I had always tuned out my mother when she began talking about the Bible, so even if I had heard the verse, I wouldn't remember it.

"Well, John 3:16-17 says: 'For God so loved the world that He gave his only begotten Son, that whoever believes in Him shall not perish, but have eternal life... God did not send the Son into the world to judge the world, but that the world might be saved through Him' He wants you to choose Him, Callie, he wants all of us to choose him, but it is your choice to reject or submit to Him while He waits at the door of your heart."

"I think I like what you're saying," I said slowly, surprised to find that it was true, "but I'm not sure I'm ready to make that decision."

Sandra folded her hands in her lap. "That's okay, dear; Jesus will be there when you are ready to decide. He never gives up on us. I'll keep praying for you, and so will the prayer warriors at my church."

I left the abortion clinic relieved and uneasy at the same time. The tightly coiled spring of fear in my stomach had abated with the decision to save my baby, even if I ended putting him/her up for adoption, but a new trickling of nervousness emerged every time I thought of telling Daniel my decision. Would he stay with me or would he leave again? And did I even care if he left? Lately I had seen a different side of him than before. Or had he always been so terse and demanding? Had I been so focused on myself that I hadn't seen the real him?

Sandra's words still rattled around in my head as I entered my apartment. I turned on the lights and headed straight to the bedroom. *I think my old Bible is somewhere in here.* Crossing to the bookshelf, I scanned the titles. No Bible. I tapped my cheek, furrowing my brow. *Now where did I put it?*

As I turned to the bed, the picture of JD and I called to me from the top of the nightstand. A tingle tiptoed down my back, and I crossed to the nightstand. There on the bottom shelf was the Bible, covered in a light coat of dust. I picked it up, wiping the dust off. As I held the book, the tingling flooded into my hands.

I sat down on the bed and stared at the Bible. Having no idea where to begin, I simply let it fall open. My eyes scanned the black and white page and focused on Proverbs 3 verse 5: 'Trust in the Lord with all your heart, and do not lean on your own understanding. In all your ways acknowledge him, and he will make straight your paths.' I stared at the words and read them again. If I trusted God, would he clear the difficult path ahead of me and if he did, what would that mean?

The sound of a key in the door pulled my attention from the page. Daniel. I snapped the Bible closed and placed it on the nightstand. After a deep, steadying breath, I headed to the living room to greet him.

"What a day," Daniel stormed in and threw his coat down on the couch.

My stomach clenched, and my hands shook slightly at my side. "Oh, was it not a good day?"

He rolled his eyes. "When is it?"

I stared at him wondering if he had always been so negative or if I had been wearing blinders and was just now seeing his true colors? I tried to think back to the last time I remembered him being positive, apart from our time in the Caribbean, and drew a blank. Instead, images of quiet dinners when we were both absorbed in our work appeared. Instances when I wanted to talk to him, but his focus had been on the sports game he was watching and his body language had portrayed that now was not a good time followed. *Was I ever really in love with him or was I just in love with the thought of him?* I took a deep breath. It appeared there would be no perfect time and now was as good a time as any, "Well, I had an interesting day."

"Do you have dinner ready?" Daniel interrupted me, glancing toward the kitchen.

"What? No, I... I must have forgotten about the time, Daniel; I'm trying to tell you something that's important to me. I went to the abortion clinic today."

He sat down and grabbed the remote, not bothering to look at me. "Oh, good, did you get rid of the problem?"

I winced at the harsh words falling from his mouth. Had I sounded like that? The image of me snapping at Sandra the first day flashed in my mind, and I cringed. I didn't want to sound like that anymore. "No, I didn't. I couldn't. Daniel, I believe it is a baby."

He glared up at me, coldness in his eyes. "I thought we'd been through this already."

Rage bubbled in my core, and I bit back the words I wanted to shout at him, taking a deep breath instead. "You had, but I hadn't. I've been having dreams – dreams of this beautiful little girl who is so sad. I think she's my daughter. Then, I met one today."

"One what?" he said.

"Remember when I told you that thirty percent of women who have abortions have reproductive problems later? Well, I met one of them today. She had one abortion, and then years later when she wanted to have a baby, she couldn't."

Daniel stood, his eyes fire, and I took a step back in fear. "That doesn't mean it's going to happen to you," Daniel advanced on me, and I took another step back unsure if he was going to hit me. He never had before, but I'd never seen him this mad either. "I thought I made this clear. I don't want a baby right now, and I'm not sure I ever will."

The words stung as if they'd physically slapped me. "What?" I had always thought two children were in our perfect plan together.

He took a deep breath, and his posture relaxed. "Look, Callie, I love you, but I don't want to be a parent right now. I want to be able to do as I please, go where I want when I want, and I don't want to be held back by a child's needs."

"Do what you want? Like have more women like Shaina on the side?" I spat. "I thought she was the problem, but now I see she was just one effect of your bigger problem." My hands balled into fists at my side, and my nostrils flared. How could he be so selfish? And why hadn't she seen this side of him sooner? "I'll tell you what, I won't hold you back any longer either."

"Come on, Callie, be reasonable. You don't need a baby if you have me." He flashed his familiar charming smile and held out his hands, but I wasn't fooled this time. For the first time in a long time, I was thinking clearly.

Flexing my hands, I took another deep breath. The steadiness of my voice surprised me. "I don't need you, Daniel; I thought I did, but I'm beginning to think I need Jesus instead."

"Wait, what?" His mouth dropped open and his eyebrows drew together. "Are you becoming a Christian too?" Disdain distorted his voice.

"I'm not sure yet," I replied, crossing my arms, "but this lady I met today was a much better example to me than you have ever been."

"Well, when you come to your senses, you know where to find me," Daniel picked up his coat and jammed his arms in the sleeves, "but not while you still have a baby."

He slammed the front door behind him, and I sank down on the couch dropping my head in my hands. Questions flooded my mind. Had I done the right thing? How would I deal with this pregnancy alone? My head popped up. My mom, of course; she was always there when I needed her. I pulled out my phone, but then paused, biting my lip. I hadn't even told my mom I was pregnant yet, but surely she would still support me. I tapped the numbers and listened as it rang. "Mom, can you come over? I need to talk with you."

CHAPTER 7

*J*jumped up from the couch when the knock sounded and flew across the room to open the door. "Oh, mom, I need your help." I stepped into my mother's bewildered embrace and squeezed her tightly.

"I know something has been bothering you," my mother said as we pulled back. "Why don't you tell me what it is?"

After shutting the door, I motioned her to follow me to the couch. "I've made such a mess of things." I took a deep breath and began the sordid story. "I was feeling sorry for myself after Daniel left, and I went drinking with Lexi. Daniel's coat was hanging by my door and it was mocking me, so I didn't want to go home."

My mother shook her head in confusion, and I tried again to make the words in my head make sense as they spewed out of my mouth. "I met a guy; he seemed nice; and he made me feel pretty." I glanced up under lowered lids, "I know I shouldn't have, but I ended up staying the night at his place."

My mother sucked in her breath, "Oh, Callie."

I held up a hand. "It gets worse, mom. Daniel contacted

me while I was on vacation, and I agreed to give him another shot."

I hadn't thought my mother's eyes could get any wider, but they did. Still, she said nothing, letting me continue the story.

"Anyway, after we got back, I started getting sick. I thought it was food poisoning or something, but, mom, I went to a doctor, and I'm pregnant."

My mother's face froze, and her posture stiffened. I couldn't tell what was going on in her head. I waited for a minute, but she remained silent, so I continued, "Daniel wanted me to get an abortion."

She gasped and brought her hand to her mouth. "Tell me you didn't, Callie. Even though I wouldn't encourage a pregnancy out of wedlock, I would never want you to terminate it."

My chin trembled, "I was going to, but then I started researching the procedure and having dreams of this beautiful little girl, and I almost changed my mind. Then Daniel seemed to make so much sense about timing, and I went to the clinic, but I still wasn't sure; the final straw that changed my mind was Sandra."

"Sandra? What does she have to do with this?"

"She sits outside the abortion clinic, mom. She told me her story, and I couldn't go through with it. Then she said you asked her to pray for me after Daniel left. She's been praying for me for weeks"

"Thank heavens she was," my mother sighed. "So, is Daniel gone for good this time?"

I nodded and dropped my eyes, still battling the embarrassment of being conned. "I started to see his true personality, and I didn't like it. He was so callous, and he told me I had to choose between him and the baby, so I chose the baby."

"I'm glad, Callie." She squeezed my hands. "You may have made some mistakes, but that decision was very smart. Now, you need to find the father and tell him. He deserves to know, too."

I blinked in surprise. The thought of telling Brent had never occurred to me. It was too embarrassing to think about, but I supposed my mother was right. He did deserve to know. "I drove from his apartment the next morning, so his cross streets are still in my GPS, and I think I would remember his apartment. I'll go tomorrow."

"Don't go alone, and let's pray for God's hand to guide this situation from now on," my mother suggested.

I nodded, suddenly deciding that what I wanted more than anything was God in control of my life. "I think I'm ready now, mom; can you tell me how to pray to accept Jesus as my savior?"

"It would be my pleasure," she said, hugging me.

*A*fter my mother had gone, I plodded into the bedroom. *I wonder if she'll visit again tonight.* A smile tugged at my lips at the thought. If she came tonight, surely the dream would mirror the peace and happiness that I was feeling. As I brushed my teeth, I stared at my reflection in the bathroom mirror. Did I look a little different? I sure felt different. Now I understood why JD and Sandra had seemed so content. They must feel this same peace that was flowing through my veins. Why had I waited so long to accept God?

After I finished in the bathroom, I changed into pajamas and climbed into bed. I picked up the Bible, no longer covered in dust and spied the picture of JD. Turning it over, I read the message again. JD had been praying for me, too. *It can't be a coincidence, all those people praying for me at the same time.* I touched his face, feeling a tiny pang of regret. If only I hadn't let Daniel back in, maybe something would have happened with JD. I wondered if I would ever get another chance with him. With a small sigh, I replaced the picture and turned back to the Bible.

I turned the thin pages, realizing I still wasn't sure how to read the Bible with purpose. The word 'womb' caught my eye, and I stopped. "Before I formed you in the womb I knew you, before you were born I set you apart; I appointed you as a prophet to the nations." Jeremiah 1:5. What did that mean? I didn't feel like a prophet. What would I prophesy about? I filed the question in the back of my mind to ask my mother or Sandra about later and replaced Bible on the nightstand. Turning out the light, I placed my hands on my belly and pictured the life that was inside. Was it a girl as I had dreamed before? "Lord, whatever gender, please let this baby be healthy and help me to be a good mother."

$\mathcal{I}$ woke and glanced around; the field of daisies surrounded me again. I held a hand up to my eyes to shield the bright sunlight, and warmth flowed from my heart. The little blond angel frolicked through the flowers. She turned and smiled at me, then ran toward me. I scooped her up in my arms and breathed in her fresh scent as I whirled her around. She was older again this time.

The little girl placed two tiny hands on my face causing sheer joy to plummet through my body. "Thank you, mommy, thank you for choosing life for me."

I hugged the girl closer and caressed her soft hair. "I'm sorry I ever thought of ending your life before it began; I hope you can forgive me."

"Of course, mommy," the girl giggled. "Now, let's go get daddy." She wiggled out of my arms as I looked around.

"Who's daddy?" I asked.

"You'll see," the little girl called and ran towards a wide tree that I hadn't noticed before. As the girl neared it, an arm shot out and grabbed her hand. The tinkle of laughter carried on the wind and I held my breath, waiting for the face to appear from behind the tree.

Before the face became visible, an incessant beeping filled the air. As I turned to find the noise, the dream world shattered and my eyes opened to my bedroom. I pounded the bed in frustration. If only I'd had a few more minutes.

I found Brent's apartment without too much trouble and stood outside his door, paper in hand. I ran my empty palm down my jeans and stared at the door. Would he even remember me?

"You have to knock," Lexi said, nudging my elbow.

I smiled at Lexi, who had agreed to come after I told her the whole situation. I was pretty sure it was because Lexi felt guilty, but I was still thankful for the moral support in case the situation took an undesirable turn. I took a deep breath, calming the acid churning in my stomach, "I know." Bringing my hand up to the door, I knocked and waited, hoping that he wouldn't be home, but a lock clicked and the door swung open.

Brent stood in the doorway, clad in a pair of cut-off shorts and a white tank top, commonly referred to as a wife-beater, though I had never liked the name.

He looked from me to Lexi and smiled. "Well hey there, pretty ladies." Leaning against the doorframe, he tucked his hands in his cargo shorts' pockets. "Long time, no see."

I chewed the inside of my lip, swallowing the disgust building in my mouth. "Hi Brent; you're probably wondering what we're doing here."

"You back for seconds?" he winked at me.

I cringed and closed my eyes. *What did I ever see in this guy?* "Um, no. I'm here because I'm pregnant, and I thought you should know. I'm pretty sure you're the father due to the timing."

His swagger sobered up; he stood straighter and took a step back. "What?"

"Don't worry, I'm not asking for anything. You don't even have to be in the child's life, but I thought the proper thing to do was to tell you."

His face mottled with color as his nostrils flared. "I don't want anything to do with a baby."

"I'm not asking for anything from you," I sighed and rolled my eyes, "I just thought you might want to know."

He held out his hands as if warding off evil. "You do what you want, but don't come asking me for any child support."

My temper flared, and I sucked in my lips to keep it in check. "I won't, but I was hoping you could sign this." I thrust out the paper I had been holding in my hand.

"What is this?" he narrowed his eyes as he scanned it.

"It's the termination of your parental rights. It keeps you from having to pay child support, but also says you can't come back later and try to take the baby."

"Fine, whatever." He signed the paper in the appropriate spot, shoved it back at me, and slammed the door in our faces.

"Well that went well," Lexi smirked.

I grimaced, shaking my head, "Come on; let's get out of here."

CHAPTER 8

*J*D adjusted his dark blue tie in the bathroom mirror. He smoothed his hair back and patted his suit coat one more time. This ten o'clock meeting could open up an entirely new chapter in his life; one he had been thinking about and working on for a few years now. He took a deep breath and exited the bathroom.

The board room doors were closed when he arrived, which gave time for the kernel of unease in his stomach to grow. He knew most of the board members, but that didn't mean they would go for his idea. "Lord, send me the words and help them to see," JD whispered as he pulled the door open.

A large dark wooden table and thirteen black leather chairs were the only pieces of furniture in the almost entirely beige room. The members of the board occupied twelve of the chairs, and JD took a breath as twenty-four eyes regarded him. He sat in the remaining empty chair at the near end of the table and cleared his throat, "Welcome members of the board; I know this is a special session, but it's been weighing on my heart, and I feel like now is the time to move forward."

The members nodded telling JD to continue. "As you know, when my father built this company, one of his stipulations for success was that we always try to help those who are in need. As I watch the news each night, I feel like our country is in greater need now than ever before in a lot of areas, but the one that has been on my heart lately is crisis pregnancies. I'm not sure if my father ever told you my story, but I was adopted, and I've been feeling a need to set up a crisis pregnancy center that will specialize in adoption along with helping pregnant women find resources they need."

A few eyebrows went up at this news, but the other faces remained stoic. They were waiting for the details.

"My biological mother was too young when she became pregnant with me, and without my father's help, I don't think I'd be here today. He shared God's love with her and helped her find the resources she needed to carry me to term and put me up for adoption."

One of the women sniffed and dabbed her eyes.

"I sense that God is calling me to be that same voice for other women, and that is why I am asking for the board to help me fund a pregnancy counseling center in Texas, which I hope will be the first of many to come."

Fred, the longest standing member, leaned forward. With his white hair and bushy beard, he had often reminded JD of Santa Claus. "Why Texas?"

JD folded his hands on the table top. "Well, as you know, our culture is pretty divided on this issue, and not all places would be welcoming of a center like ours. Texas tends to be one of the more conservative states in that regard, and I'm hopeful that the community there will be more receptive. I am thinking we could set up our first center in Mesquite, which is outside of the Dallas Metroplex. I believe that location will attract many women, but it's still far enough outside the city limits that I hope the more liberal communities of the metroplex will leave it alone."

"I assume you have some specific property in mind?" Terry, another long-term board member, asked as he stroked his dark brown beard.

JD nodded, "Yes, I have checked out a few possibilities online and narrowed it down to three, but I'd like to fly out and inspect them in person. I have contacted a local realtor there, and he's offered to line up showings."

"And who will be managing this clinic?" Paul, the youngest board member, inquired. Paul was only a few years older than JD and head of the finance committee so JD knew that he was thinking about the dollar signs.

JD drew his shoulders back and let out a deep breath knowing this could be the make or break point. If they didn't feel the company could run without him, they might say no, but he had to chance it as he really felt God calling him to set up the center personally. "I will, at least to begin with. God's plan on that part isn't as clear yet, though I have no doubt he will reveal it in time. You all can manage the company while I'm away. You've done a great job so far. So... what do you think?"

"Why don't you step outside and give us a minute?" Fred asked.

JD's throat dried up. He had known the decision would require a decision, but he had thought he would be there for it. Nodding, he turned and stepped into the hall. The door swung shut behind him and he leaned his head back against the wall. "I've done my part, Lord. The rest is up to you," he whispered. A feeling of peace covered his head and slowly trickled down the rest of his body.

A moment later, the door opened and Fred motioned him back inside the room. All eyes were trained on him once again as Fred clapped a hand on his shoulder, much like his father used to when he was growing up.

"Well, I think I speak for everyone," Fred began, "when I say that your father would be very proud of you, and that we are happy to extend the money you will need for this project." Fred was the first to extend a hand for JD to shake, but the rest of the board members stood and joined the line, voicing their congratulations as well. The final kernel of unease fizzled out, and JD sent a silent prayer of thanks heavenward.

When he returned to his apartment that afternoon, the realization of the decision finally hit him. He looked around at everything he was going to have to pack. He had no idea how long it would take to get a center up and running, so he was planning on putting most of his items in storage and moving to Texas at least temporarily. Of course he had a few things he had to wrap up here first, including finishing out his current lease, which bought him a couple of months.

He hated the thought of losing his rent-controlled apartment, but he was no longer sure New York was where he was supposed to be. Even before he had met Callie, he had been feeling restless, like he was being called elsewhere, but after meeting her, the feeling had intensified. When she had mentioned she lived in Texas, the place where he had often thought of opening his first center, he had thought maybe it was a sign that they were meant for each other, but then her fiancé had re-entered the picture and shattered that dream.

He picked up the picture of the two of them he had placed on his bookshelf and perused her face again. Though he knew it was a long shot, he had realized long ago never to assume something was too big for God, and as she kept popping into his mind he had to assume that their paths would meet again.

CHAPTER 9

*A*s I dressed for work the following Monday, I was still smiling and felt lighter than I had in a long time. The meeting with Brent had gone about as good as could be expected, but I had the paper signed now, so he couldn't come back and try to take the child. That in itself gave me a measure of peace, but I'd also gotten the chance to share my story with Lexi over lunch. While Lexi hadn't been convinced she needed Jesus, she had agreed to try church with me the next day.

At church, I'd been able to thank Sandra for playing such a pivotal role in my life, and I'd been able to introduce Lexi to her. I didn't know why, but I had this feeling that people who met Sandra eventually accepted Jesus. She just had this air about her. Sandra, ever the enigmatic one, had smiled and given the credit to God, but I knew my decision had given her heart some joy.

My life was not turning out the way I had planned, but I was pretty content with where it was going so far. The only regret I had was JD. I couldn't change the past, but I now believed that prayer could change lives and so every morning and every evening I prayed for God to send JD back into my life.

I spared a look in the hall mirror on my way out the door and smiled at the change I saw even in myself.

"Well, what happened to you?" Tina asked as I approached the desk.

My smile deepened at the thought that my transformation was so evident. "Follow me into my office, and I'll tell you." Tina's brow rose, her curiosity piqued.

With the door shut, I spilled the story of my trip, my breakup, and my pregnancy, ending with my acceptance of Jesus into my heart.

"Oh Callie, I'm so excited for you. I've been praying for you since I started working here," Tina wiped tears from her eyes.

My eyes widened. "You have?"

"Of course," Tina nodded, "I want you to be in Heaven with me when I get there. I had an all-night prayer vigil with the Lord the night I suspected your pregnancy. I was concerned you were so focused on your career that you would choose an abortion."

I blinked as Tina's words sank in, "I can't believe how close I came to doing just that, and I can't believe how many people were praying for me when I didn't even know what was happening. I hope I too can become a prayer warrior like you and the others who have been praying for me."

"I think God has big things in store for you, Callie," Tina smiled. "Now tell me more about this handsome man you met there."

I sighed. "I wish I could, but I never even got his last name. I messed that up so badly."

"Don't worry about it. I thought I had messed things up when I first met Gary, my husband. I told him I wasn't interested and tried to date his best friend. He ended up moving across the country, but eventually he came back and God brought us back together. I think if you are patient, you'll find that God can do anything. Just remember to pray about it and be open to God's prompting."

I nodded and hugged the assistant that was quickly becoming a friend. Next on my list was Lexi. Though she had gone to church, I could tell she still wasn't ready. I'd call her today and see if she wanted to do lunch again. With that settled, I sat down and faced the pile of work on my desk.

CHAPTER 10

*T*hree Months Later

*T*he taxi dropped JD off in front of the bed and breakfast he had researched online. The pictures had not done justice to the quaint Victorian house. The steps creaked a little under his footsteps, but the porch was clean and homey. Two wooden rocking chairs sat in front of the large window.

He pushed open the cream-colored door and stepped into the homey front entrance. A small brown desk filled the area just to the left of the carpeted stairs. The older woman manning the desk looked up as the door closed behind him. Her dark hair had some strands of grey, but she was still a beautiful woman.

"Welcome to the Parson House," she said. "Do you have a reservation?"

"Yes, under the name of Peterson."

She tapped a few keys in her computer and then flashed

a smile at him. His breath caught in his throat. Her smile reminded him of Callie's the day they had taken pictures at the falls. Of course lately nearly every woman he saw reminded him of Callie in some way or another.

"Yes, room 202. I hope you'll enjoy your stay. Do you need help taking anything to your room?"

He shook his head, both in answer and in an effort to clear the image of Callie from it. She smiled again and handed him a key.

"Up the stairs and first room on your right. The bathroom is just across the hall."

Thanking her, he grabbed his bag and stepped up the stairway. The room was decorated in browns and golds, giving it a masculine feel. A single queen-sized bed filled most of the room, but a small dresser hugged one wall, and a squat nightstand sat next to the bed. It wasn't much, but it only had to be home for a few days until he found an apartment.

He unzipped his bag and pulled out his Bible. The realtor was showing him three buildings tomorrow and he wanted to be sure his mind was clear and focused on his purpose.

CHAPTER 11

"Mom, are you ready? I'm hungry." I patted the belly that was just starting to protrude past my pants. Luckily, I was still able to work out, though modified, so I hadn't gained too much weight.

"Why don't we just eat here?" my mother said, gesturing to the small dining room to the left.

I rolled my eyes. "Mom, you eat here nearly every night. Let's go out somewhere tonight."

She shot a glance upstairs before sighing and gathering her purse. "Okay, I was just hoping the handsome new check-in might be at dinner. I think you'd like him."

"Mom, I don't have time for a man right now and really, who's going to want a pregnant one? He'd have to put up with all my cravings and mood swings and get nothing in return." That wasn't entirely true. I did want a man, but only one specific man that I had no idea how to find.

"A good Christian man would understand," my mother insisted.

"And I'll find one, but right now I'm a little swamped with work and preparing for a kid."

Though my words were confident, as we stepped into the evening air, I did wonder when God would provide the perfect man. I had been praying for months, and while I wasn't getting discouraged exactly, I was beginning to wonder how much longer I would have to wait. I knew it was a long shot that I'd ever see JD again, but surely there had to be more men like him that God could send.

*J*D had scoped out three buildings and settled on a small office building in the middle of town. It seemed to have everything doctors would need; it was centrally located; and it was affordable.

JD surveyed the rooms one more time and nodded. "I'd like to pray about it, but I'm pretty sure this is the one I'm going to want. Can you draw up an offer for me Scott?"

"Of course, but do you think God cares about which property you buy?"

"God cares about everything I do, and if I decide this without him, the business may not succeed."

Scott smirked and scoffed, "Wow, you must take this God thing seriously."

JD turned serious eyes on Scott. "I do. God has had a hand in my life – from day one, and when I follow Him, things always go better for me."

Scott tilted his head, "Can I ask what you mean?" There was no condescension in the words, just an honest question.

JD smiled and laughed. "Where do I begin?" He pointed to a nearby table with chairs, and the two men sat. "Well, I guess at the beginning. My mom was 15 when she became pregnant with me. When that happened, everyone told her to have an abortion because she was so young and having a baby would ruin her life. One day, she met my father at the coffee shop where she worked. As he had opportunity, he spoke to her about God. Then he told her how he and my mother wanted a baby more than anything but couldn't get pregnant. One day, after several conversations, he invited her to church and explained to her who Jesus was and what He did for her. She accepted Christ as her Savior and decided to let my father and mother adopt me.

"That was the first time God intervened in my life. Later on, when I was twelve, I was hit by a car. The accident should have killed me, but after a policeman helped me up, I barely had a scratch on me. I gave my life to God that very day and committed to follow him from then on. However, years later, when I got to college, I met a girl. I knew she wasn't a Christian and that God didn't want me involved with her, but I ignored Him. Soon thereafter, my life fell apart when I got involved in drugs, drinking, and partying. Then I flunked out of college and of course the girl I fell in love with, well, she ended up breaking my heart. At that point, I was at the end of my rope; realizing I could not effectively govern my life; I went back to God and then joined my father's company. As I began to pray for its success, it grew in size. Next, I began to pray for something bigger to be involved in and God put a calling on my heart to establish pregnancy counseling centers. Therefore, given my level of success in prayer so far, I'm going to pray about this location and ask God to bless it."

Scott sat back in his chair and raised his left eyebrow. "So, because you had one bad relationship you think God was punishing you?"

JD smiled and shook his head. "No, He wasn't punishing me. God has a plan for all believers and when we don't follow his plan, we won't receive the blessings He wants to give us. I decided that I'd rather be blessed than suffer from fighting against Him. Besides, I want to honor Him in all that I do."

"So, are you saying that if you follow God, he will make you rich?" Scott placed his hands on his knees and leaned forward.

JD laughed. "No, I said blessed, not rich. Being blessed isn't about money; blessings can come in many ways - for the rich and poor alike. The company I represent is one blessing; the feeling of peace I have when I wake up every morning is another. God can and does bless His children in so many glorious ways one cannot begin to count them all. We need to look for them to see what they are."

"Well, being blessed does sound good to me," Scott leaned back in his chair. "But how do you know when God is calling you? I've been to church a few times, but God never spoke to me."

"God works in many different ways to call people to salvation. He works through preaching, through print, radio and TV media, and through a one on one witness from a believer. Unbelievers come to Christ when they are convicted of their sin through one of these means and realize they need Him to be their Savior because they cannot save themselves.

"Once a person becomes a Christian, the Holy Spirit, who fills the hearts of believers in Christ, often uses a still, small voice when He speaks, so a Christian has to read the word of God, pray for guidance and be quiet long enough to sense His leading. That's the hard part. Sometimes God even moves in your life by reminding you of something you need to do. It might be something your mind keeps coming back to, like starting counseling centers has been for me. I've been thinking about this goal and looking into it for a few years now and even though I couldn't do anything about it previously, the thought has always been there."

Scott nodded and rubbed his chin with his right hand. "I

think I'd like to know more about what it's like to be a Christian. Can we get together in a day or two for coffee?"

Warmth flooded JD, and he smiled. "Of course, I'll be staying in town until the project is done. Would you like to meet on Thursday, say at 10 am, at that coffee shop right over there?" He pointed at the Cup O'Joe across the street.

Scott opened his satchel and grabbed his schedule book. He flipped a few pages and nodded "Sure, it looks free, so I'll see you then."

*S*ighing, I pushed open the door to my apartment. It had been another long day, and though I didn't stand all day, my feet still managed to ache by the time I got home and tonight they were throbbing fiercely. Dropping my purse by the couch, I shuffled into the kitchen to boil some water for tea.

When the tea kettle whistled, I turned the stove off and poured the water into my cup of tea. Enjoying the warmth, I carried the cup to the living room and lounged on the brown suede couch to rest my weary feet and read. I set the tea cup down on the end table and picked up my Bible. The crinkling sound of the thin pages brought a smile to my face.

As the pages separated, my eyes landed on Ecclesiastes 3. "To everything there is a season, and a time to every purpose under the heaven: 2 A time to be born, and a time to die; a time to plant, and a time to pluck up that which is planted; 3 A time to kill, and a time to heal; a time to break down, and a time to build up; 4 A time to weep, and a time to laugh; a time to mourn, and a time to dance; 5 A time to cast away stones, and a time to gather stones together; a time to embrace, and a time to refrain from embracing; 6 A time to get, and a time to lose; a time to keep, and a time to cast away; 7 A time to rend, and a time to sew; a time to keep silence, and a time to speak; 8 A time to love, and a time to hate; a time of war, and a time of peace."

The words reminded me of a time months ago when JD had told me that everything happens for a reason. I hadn't believed him then, but I knew now that I probably wouldn't have given my life to God if I hadn't gotten pregnant. He had taken that mistake she made and turned it into something wonderful. As I rubbed my belly, I thought back to the time I had spent with JD. *I wonder what he's doing now and if I'll ever see him again.* I sent up a short prayer for JD wherever he was and then resumed my reading.

CHAPTER 12

I entered the doctor's office at 9am. Butterflies tumbled in my stomach; today was the day I would find out for sure the gender of the baby.

"Morning Callie," the perky brunette receptionist greeted me.

"Good morning," I smiled back, signing in on the sheet.

"Are you ready for the ultrasound?" the receptionist asked.

I touched my stomach, smiling as the baby moved against my hand. He or she had started moving a few weeks ago, and I still couldn't get over the sensation. "I sure am." *Though I'm pretty sure I already know the gender of this one.* I sat down in a brown chair and waited to be called back in the room.

"Are we waiting on anyone?" the technician asked when I was called back.

"No," I raised my shirt and lay back on the cold hospital bed. "It's just me."

"Okay," the blond technician pushed her glasses up her freckled nose. She grabbed the tube of gel from the tray by the bed. "Sorry, this will be a little cold." I flinched as the cold gel hit my stomach. The technician grabbed the wand and began spreading the gel around. "So first, I'm going to take pictures, and then maybe we can determine gender if you want, and if this little one cooperates."

Grainy black and white images began to appear on the screen and I drew in a quiet breath. While I wasn't sure what each picture was, I could easily pick out the baby's head.

I glanced at the technician and weighed whether the woman would be offended by the question I wanted to pose, "Can I ask you a question?"

"You want to know what everything is?" the technician laughed. "Everyone does."

"Well, yes, but that wasn't my question. It's kind of personal I guess, but I wanted to know how anyone can look at an ultrasound that clearly shows a baby like this and then choose an abortion."

The technician stopped for a minute, lowered her voice, and leaned in. "It's not my area, but I honestly don't know either. You see this here?" She pointed to a grayish part at the top of the picture, "That's your baby's brain, fully formed and full of pain receptors like ours. And here?" she moved the wand, "baby's feet. Ten perfect toes by the way. I know some people say fetus, but I've done so many of these; they are all babies to me."

I smiled at the young blond. "Don't worry, I won't tell your secret," she winked.

"Would you like to know gender now?" the technician smiled back.

My heart sped up as I nodded eagerly. "Well, I'm 99% sure it's a girl, but I wouldn't mind the verification."

The wand circled some more and I held my breath. "Well, it's always a little harder to determine with girls, but I'd say your inclination is correct."

"Does everything look okay? I mean is she okay?"

The technician patted my arm, "She looks great, and I'll print out some pictures you can take with you."

As she stepped out the room, I wiped the rest of the gel off my stomach and returned my shirt to its proper position. Relief flooded me with the knowledge that the baby was okay. My hand touched my stomach again. *A girl. I knew it would be a girl.* The technician re-entered with several black and white photos of the little life that was inside me. As I held them, a warm sensation spread from my head all the way to my toes. I studied each one carefully, marveling at how much I could see. Hands, feet, heart, brain, profile. There was no doubt in my mind now; this was a baby. My baby. My Hope.

*A*bout the time I was beginning my ultrasound, JD was meeting with Scott at a nearby coffee shop.

"So what did the big man upstairs say?" Scott joked as he poured his tall frame into an empty chair. The shop was relatively slow, so they had their choice of seats.

JD smiled and sat across from him. "Well, I prayed, I listened, and I'm 98% certain this is the right building for us." He lifted his cup and took a sip of his coffee.

"Only 98%? Why not 100?" Scott cocked an eyebrow.

"I would never confess to know 100% of God's plan. There is still a lot of my old ways in my head that try to mislead me, so even though I try hard to make sure I'm hearing what He is saying, I can never be completely sure I'm not at the same time influencing myself a little."

Scott raised his eyebrow and leaned forward. "You really are into this God thing, aren't you?"

JD smiled and took a sip of his coffee. He could tell that Scott thought he was a little nuts, but he was used to that.

"God has been there every time I needed him. And besides, it's nice to know where I'm going when I die."

Scott blinked and took a sip of his coffee, "What do you mean?"

JD set his cup down and leaned back in his chair a little. "Well Scott, there's only one of two places any of us can go to after death. Those who have a relationship with Jesus will get to fellowship with him in Heaven - forever. Those who don't . . . well, the Bible says that when they stand before God He will say: 'Depart from Me, I never knew you' and that statement will earn a non-believer a one-way ticket to a place that is nowhere near heaven. It's a place where men and women will forever be separated from Him."

Scott's mouth fell open before he could catch himself. "Do you really believe in a Heaven and Hell, JD?"

"I do, and believe me, the Bible's description of Hell is a place no one would want to go and that's why we believers work so hard to tell people about Jesus."

Scott narrowed his eyes and glanced around the coffee shop. JD followed his gaze, but the coffee shop was just getting busy and no one seemed to be listening. "So, you're saying, if I don't choose Jesus, I condemn myself to Hell and you are trying to help me prevent that by telling me about him?"

JD nodded and picked up his drink again. "I think everyone deep down inside knows that God exists, Scott. I mean, how else did we get here? Scientists don't even buy the whole amoeba theory anymore because they can't recreate it. No one can because God made us in His image, according to the book of Genesis. So, whether anyone talks to you about Jesus or not, you choose to reject Him by default, because you do not follow your suspicion and try to find out about Him for yourself. You did not pursue the truth to see if He exists. You simply choose to ignore Him and continue to follow the world's thinking on the matter and thereby, you turn your back on God and you must live with the consequence of that decision."

Scott leaned back, sipping his coffee. JD could tell that his words were having an effect, but he wasn't sure what effect. He wished, not for the first time, that he could read minds. "So, are you telling me that almost everyone today is wrong?" Scott finally said.

JD held up his hands, palms out. "Look, I'm not to judge; only God can do that. I've done a lot of things in my past that I'm not proud of, but what's going on in our country today is not what God wants for America. As a nation, we removed Him from schools and kids started killing each other. We allowed sex education to be taught in schools, and now we hand out condoms instead of teaching kids to wait until after marriage to have sex. Scott, this country was founded as 'one nation under God, indivisible,' but we have become divided because we as Christians haven't been standing up against the atrocities that have been occurring over the last several decades of time. We let them continue and hoped that somebody else would do something about it, but no one has. God destroyed earlier cities for practicing things we praise today, and I don't know how much longer He'll keep watching all of the evil we are not confronting before He feels the need to cleanse the Earth again."

Scott gripped his cup tighter. His eyes darted around again. JD's words were obviously making him uncomfortable "You don't really believe he will wipe the Earth out, do you?"

"Actually, I believe He can and someday will. You see, God had the Bible written to tell us about Him; about what has happened, and will yet happen. While He hasn't told us when the end will come, He has told us to be ready for what will precede it- the rapture of God's children – the removal of believers from the earth will occur first. Then the world will be thrown into seven years of horrible tribulation. After that, there will be one thousand years of peace on earth because Jesus – the Son of God will for that time period reign over everything. God did reveal some signs in the Bible that let us know when the end time is getting close and some of those signs are happening now. There's a lot of debate about the signs and what they mean, but one or two that are very clear are that the world will have the power to destroy itself, which we do now with all our nuclear weapons, and there will be worldwide communication because, at one point, two prophets of God will be killed and will lie in the streets for three and a half days for the whole world to see them.

"Now the world hasn't been introduced to these prophets yet, but we're technologically advanced enough that when they die, they will be seen by everyone in the world at once. Plus, Christians will be persecuted, and that also is happening now. Finally, Jesus said that once these signs begin, the generation of that day will not pass away before He returns to govern the whole earth. Now, of course, we aren't sure how long a generation is in God's eyes, but it seems that if these prophecies can now be fulfilled - they soon will be."

The color drained from Scott's face, and his shoulders dropped as leaned forward. "So what happens to the rest of the population when the believers are taken from the world?"

"Well, no one knows for sure, but did you ever read the Left Behind books?"

"I'm not much of a reader," Scott admitted, "more of a football fan."

JD could tell Scott was trying to make light of the situation. "Hey, I like football as much as the next person, but this is about eternity. I'll tell you about the books someday or loan you mine; I tend to think something along those lines is what will happen. First, many will die in crashes because driving believers will disappear. Airplanes will spin out of control or crash for the same reason. Second, those who live will see other signs. They will see a man claiming to be God and doing miraculous things, and they will have to decide whether to take his mark on their body or chose to follow God instead."

Scott scratched his chin. "So, people could still get saved during that time?"

"I believe so, but Scott, please don't wait. What if you are left behind and you die because believers who were responsible for you have disappeared? That's a lot to hedge a bet on."

Scott nodded and sipped his coffee. His eyes stayed focused on the beige cup in his hands and JD couldn't gauge his reaction. He held his tongue as the seconds ticked by, giving the man time to think.

"You're right." Scott raised his eyes. The humor was gone from them, replaced with a serious expression. "You've definitely given me a lot to think about."

Relief flooded JD. This was always the hardest part of being a believer – sharing with non-believers. He didn't like telling people they might be wrong, but he didn't want their souls on his conscience either. It had taken him years, but he was finally feeling more comfortable sharing the word. "Look, let's sign the papers, and then why don't you find a church nearby and we'll go together this Sunday?"

"Deal," Scott agreed.

I tapped the steering wheel, impatient at the long line. Rotating my wrist, I glanced at the face of my watch. Ten minutes left. I was going to be late, and I hated being late. If I wasn't sandwiched between two cars, I would have just backed up and foregone the drink, but a car had pulled in right behind me, and now I had no place to go. My thumbnail returned to my teeth. I had to kick this nervous gesture before I chewed my nails completely off. Maybe if I texted Tina, she could stall until I returned.

As I reached for the phone in my purse beside me, two men exited the coffee shop. The broad shoulders and chin length hair grabbed my attention and my breath caught in my throat. It couldn't be.

Forgetting the phone, I craned my head to follow the man as he walked to the cars in the parking lot. He had the same gait, the same grace, but what on earth would he be doing in my town?

A horn blared behind me, returning my attention to the line I was in. The car ahead had moved, and I inched mine up to fill the empty space. I glanced back for the man, but he had disappeared into a car, and I had no idea which one.

Frustration roared again, and I pounded the steering wheel with open palms. I couldn't lose him again.

The line moved again, and I forked over my money, no longer caring about the steaming chai tea I placed in the cup holder before exiting the drive-thru and returning to work.

"You're late," Tina hissed as I approached the desk.

I slapped my forehead. I had forgotten to text Tina and ask her to cover. "I know; have they started?"

A smile broke out on Tina's face. "No, I told them your appoint ran late, but they're waiting for you."

"Thank you," I mouthed and turned to the hallways that led to the conference room.

"Wait, don't take your drink."

I had forgotten the tea was even in my hand. "Here, it's a chai tea. Enjoy."

Tina blinked in surprise, but took the outstretched cup, and I continued to the board room.

The other members of the small team were already inside. Issuing a quick apology, I pulled out the open chair and sat down. The stiff back made it impossible to get comfortable. Discreetly, I tried to adjust and switch positions.

Jeff, the man heading the team, began speaking, but his words flew by my ears. My thoughts were still on the man at the coffee shop.

There was a chance that it hadn't been JD. After all, the country was huge and last I knew he was in New York, but if it had been him. . . If it had, I had to find a way to run across him again, but how?

"Does that work for you, Callie?"

The sound of my name cut through my interior monologue, and my face heated as I realized I had not been listening. "I'm so sorry; I was distracted. Can you repeat?"

Jeff sighed. He had never been a fan of mine, probably because I had once beaten him at a case and then rubbed it in his face – I should apologize for that. He had fought to keep me off this case, but hadn't won. "I asked if you could handle researching previous precedent."

"Yes," I nodded, determined to keep my mind on the discussion for the rest of the meeting. "I can handle the research."

"Perfect." Jeff turned his attention from me and continued detailing his plan. To keep my mind focused, I retrieved a pen and a small notepad from my bag and took notes on the rest of the meeting.

"Thank you for covering," I whispered to Tina at the end of the day. Tina was busy putting the work in neat little stacks for the next day, which was one reason I loved having her as an assistant.

I'm not sure Tina had always been so organized, but when she had first started working for me, I had insisted that everything always be in neat piles. It was the only way I could work, and Tina had promptly conformed without complaint.

"You're welcome." Tina placed the last paper and then neatened the pile before looking up. "Thanks for the tea. What happened by the way?"

"I think I ran into my past."

Tina's face clouded over and she crossed her arms. If this was the face she used on her children, I could see why they behaved so well the few times they had been in the office. "Don't tell me it was Daniel."

"No." I stole a furtive glance to the left and right to make sure no office gossip lingered nearby. "I think I saw JD."

Tina squealed and then clapped a hand to her mouth as I shushed her. "Sorry," she said softly. "Are you sure?"

"I'm not. I just saw him for a moment while I was waiting in line at the drive-thru – what a dumb idea that was – but that build was hard to forget." My face warmed at the thought of JD's muscular frame and the solidness of his chest. "Now, I just have to find a way to find him again."

"Do you know what he does? Maybe we could check out some of the similar companies and see if he is doing work for them here."

I mentally kicked myself for my previous self-absorbed attitude. "I don't," I sighed. "All I ever knew was that he owned a business." Why hadn't I asked him more questions about himself?

Tina's eyes held the same question, but she was nice enough not to voice it out loud. "Let's pray then that God finds a way for you to meet. After all, if it is JD, the Lord brought him here."

Tina had the knack for always finding the positive. Though I was growing daily, I was still floundering in some areas and seeing the silver lining was one of them, but Tina and my mother seemed to have it down. I hoped one day it would become second nature for me as well.

After another secretive glance – praying at work wasn't forbidden, but it could cause problems – we whispered a prayer and then walked out of the building together. I waved goodbye as we separated at the parking lot. Tonight was my mother's night off from the inn, so she was making dinner at home. Though not a bad cook myself, I still loved my mother's cooking. It reminded me of a simpler time in life.

My mother's old Ford Taurus was in the driveway of the small yellow house when I pulled up. An old tattered rope swing still hung lopsided from a branch of the sole tree in the front yard. I remembered always begging my mother to go outside and swing on that swing. I hadn't known it then, but I realized now it had been my coping mechanism after my parents split. On the swing, I could pretend to fly to another world where daddies never left and mommies never cried.

I parked the car and stepped out. The grass covering the rest of the yard was a faded yellow and crunchy under my feet as I walked up to the front door. I'd have to remind my mother to water the yard or see if I could afford to hire someone to do it all the time.

Twisting the front handle of the faded white front door, I stepped inside. The smell of Mexican seasonings flew through the air, mingling with the sound of meat browning in a skillet. That meant burritos or tacos, my favorites.

I closed the door behind me and crossed through the living room to the bright airy kitchen. Mother had decorated it a few years ago in a country type flavor with blue gingham prints and pale yellow cupboards. I was more a fan of contemporary style with dark cabinets and lighter countertops, but my mother had been insistent.

"Hey honey, how was work?" My mother turned from the stove at the sound of my footsteps. The house was so old that many of the floorboards creaked. It was impossible to sneak up on someone. I had found that out the one time I had tried to sneak out to a party in High school. My mother had been up before I even hit the front door, and I had been grounded for two weeks after. I hated the floor back then, but now it brought comfort.

"It was okay. I have a new research project on my plate that is going to mean some late nights of work." I situated myself in one of the barstools, leaning back as far as I could to stretch my ever-increasing belly. People did not think about pregnant women when the made straight-backed chairs.

A line of worry etched across her face. "Are you sure you want to keep doing this job? Those long hours can be hard when you're pregnant, and they'll be impossible once she comes."

"I know mom, but I'm not sure what else to do yet. I might as well stay as long as I can because the money's good and will sure help out when Hope comes." My mother's worry had been the same one running circles through my mind. The late nights were taking a toll on my health, and I knew I couldn't continue them much longer, but not many companies were looking to hire a woman five months pregnant. Still, I kept my ears open and perused the ads daily on my break. I'd definitely have to find another job once Hope arrived, though I would definitely miss Tina.

The worry didn't fade completely from my mother's face, but she nodded and turned back to stir the meat.

I traced my finger across the ecru bar counter. "Mom, do you believe in coincidences?"

"What do you mean, honey?" With the meat at the temperature she wanted, my mother lowered the flame and turned to the bar where a cutting board held a few tomatoes and some lettuce. She picked up the knife and began slicing the ripe red fruit.

"This afternoon I could have sworn a man I met while I was in the Caribbean was at the coffee shop." I smiled, remembering the waterfall and the van ride that had allowed me to jostle against him, and a tingle ran down my spine.

"I take it you liked him."

I sighed. "I did, but I didn't realize it back then. Then Daniel called, and I was so confused that I took him back. JD, that was his name, left, and I thought I'd never see him again. But a few months ago, I found a travel book he had given me the day he left and inside was a picture of us and a note; then the other night when I was reading, I ran across a verse that reminded me of him. And today, I could have sworn he was at Cup O' Joe."

"Did you talk to him?" Mother chopped the tomato slices into squares, scraped them into a bowl, and grabbed the head of lettuce.

"No, I was in the drive thru lane, and he was getting in his car. There wasn't time." I dropped my head into my hands, all my confidence from my earlier talk with Tina fading.

"Well, I don't believe in coincidence," my mother smiled. "See, God knew us before we were born and had a plan for us, so I tend to think that God has a hand in everything that happens in our life, including things we might see as coincidences."

"That's basically what Tina said – that God brought him here, so maybe we are destined to meet again."

She smiled back at me. "What do you think Callie?"

"I think I'm going to continue to pray about it and ask God's wisdom." A wistful smile crossed my face, "but I have to say, I don't think I'd mind if JD were in my life."

As my mother chopped the lettuce, I regaled her with

stories of the few days I had spent with JD. With every detail I remembered, I felt more and more sure that my mother was right – I had met JD for a reason.

*S*unday morning, I woke up with butterflies zooming around in my stomach. Last month, I had decided to get involved at church, and this morning I was going to be singing on stage with the choir. A part of me was excited because I had always loved singing, but another part of me was still worried about what people might say. No one had said anything out loud to me, but a few people hadn't been able to keep their eyes from wandering to my left hand in search of a ring as my belly began to show. Mother and I had agreed to tell people as they asked instead of making a blanket announcement. As this would be my first time on the stage, I hoped to be a blessing and not a distraction.

The baby turned, sending a fluttering sensation through me. Lately, Hope seemed to read my moods and react to them. Placing a hand on my belly, I rubbed in a slow circle to soothe her. "I know girl, but I think it will be okay." Turning my face heavenward, I whispered a soft prayer. Peace flowed over me and the fluttering in my stomach calmed as well.

❀

*A*cross town, JD was meeting Scott at Cup O'Joe.
"Did you pick a place you'd like to try out?" JD picked up one coffee and handed it to Scott before grabbing the next one.

Scott shrugged, "Yeah, I mean I don't know much about it, but according to all the events its website listed, Mesquite View sounds interesting enough to visit and it's right down the road."

JD nodded and took a sip of his coffee. The hot liquid was perfect, one sugar and just a hint of cream. "Well, let's give it a shot. I've often found that a church either feels right or not quite your style."

The coffee shop was mostly empty, so they had their choice of table. Scott picked one by the door and JD followed him. The unease radiated off Scott in the way he never set his drink down and took a sip every few seconds. JD wanted to allay his fears, but he knew that sometimes it was best just to be quiet and let God work.

However, when Scott finished his drink first and began turning the cup in slow circles on the table, JD decided his energy would be better spent in moving.

"Is the church close enough to walk?" JD downed another sip, but he still had half a cup of coffee remaining. Sine he couldn't stomach the thought of throwing away perfectly good coffee and he was pretty sure the church would have a trash, if not some other place along the way, he decided to take the rest of his drink with him.

"I think so." Scott pulled out his phone and swiped the screen. He tapped a few times and pulled up a map. "Yes, it looks like it's right around the corner."

"Wonderful," JD said, holding the door open for Scott as he threw his empty cup away. "Let's walk."

The wind whipped leaves around them as soon as they stepped out of the wind block the restaurant had offered, and JD pulled his coat tighter around himself.

How different Texas was from New York. Fewer people crowded the streets and the sun appeared closer and warmer, even in the dead of winter. Small mesquite trees lined the sidewalk, but there weren't tall buildings obscuring his view as they strolled. JD took a breath and realized even the air smelled different.

As they turned the corner, a large brick building came

into view. The church along with its front and back parking lot covered a quarter of a block. Three large crosses sat atop the middle roof. "It's a pretty big place," JD said as they crossed the crowded parking lot. A few people milled around the front entrance conversing with each other and greeting people that approached.

An older gentleman with a bald pate but a white fluffy beard and mustache trundled their direction. He was dressed in a black suitcoat, pants, and a blue tie. JD hoped they wouldn't be too underdressed in their dress slacks and button down shirts. "Welcome," he said and handed them a program.

Another man opened the door for them, younger and with a full head of hair. JD was relieved to see he wasn't wearing a suitcoat, though he did still have on a tie. "The sanctuary is ahead, and the bathrooms are around that corner. Have a great morning."

JD nodded back, and he and Scott filed into the large sanctuary. A stage with a piano, guitars, and a drum set adorning it stretched across the front of the room and a large cross stood on the left side. White screens behind the stage and on either side flashed announcements. Instead of pews, rows of padded chairs filled the room, separated into three sections. JD led the way to an empty row on the right side and sat down. Scott followed, though his gaze was flicking from one item to the next in the large room.

JD opened the pamphlet and began reading the offerings. "Look, Scott, this place has Bible studies and a great men's group. That's one thing you want to look for in a church, because you need to find a place to get connected. They also have a worship team if you sing or play an instrument and a prayer team if you want to join."

As if on cue, people began filing onto the stage. JD hadn't noticed the rows of risers in the back, but they drew his attention as the people filed onto them. It was a large choir as the top row soon filled, then the middle row, then the bottom row began filling. At the very end of the line of people currently taking the stage was a woman with long dark hair that rippled like moonlight on the ocean.

JD's heart stopped and his breath caught. He remembered that hair, how it had smelled of flowers and vanilla and how he had longed to run his fingers through it. He blinked his eyes. Surely, it wasn't her though as the Callie he had met didn't seem like the type to be singing in the choir on Sundays. As she stepped on the riser and began to turn, he leaned forward in his seat.

"What's wrong?" Scott asked beside him.

His change in posture must have caught the man's attention. JD held his finger up. He just needed another minute. The woman turned and JD's heart shattered. He fell back against the chair back feeling as if he'd just gotten punched in the gut.

"Are you okay?"

Scott needed an explanation, but JD didn't have the words yet. He couldn't even make his mind grasp the image he was seeing; how could he explain it? He had been so sure.

The worship team had taken the stage some time in his shock, and the music began. Though it was like looking at a car crash, JD couldn't keep his eyes from returning to the woman on the bottom row.

He couldn't see the color of her eyes from here, but he knew they were green, deep like an emerald but with flecks of gold in them. They were emblazoned in his memory both from their short time together and from the countless times he had stared at the picture. She smiled and the dimple on each side of her mouth became visible. The sight both elated JD and broke his heart even further, if that was possible. He wanted to know what had happened to her, where this change had come from. He couldn't imagine that the man he had met on the last day he had seen her had inspired this change in her. The look of apprehension had been visible in her eyes even then when that arrogant man had pulled her close, staking his claim, but clearly something had happened.

Though he was no expert, the hang of her maxi dress on her otherwise thin frame displayed a protruding baby bump. Had she known back then that she was pregnant? He thought back to the double tequila he had served her the first night and the drinks she must have consumed the second night to have been so bold. She must not have. She had her faults, but she was so logical that he couldn't imagine her playing Russian Roulette with her baby's fate.

Did it happen after then? He didn't want to imagine her sharing a bed with the man who had broken her heart and upended her life, but he knew she must have. He wished he could gauge how far along she was until he realized it didn't matter. Whether she was one week or thirty-eight, she was clearly now attached to another man and therefore off the market.

Scott was still staring at him, waiting for some explanation.

"I'll tell you after the service," JD whispered, surprised that his voice wasn't shaking when the rest of him seemed to be. "Let's just enjoy the message."

JD forced his eyes to the screen farthest from Callie's face and tried to join in the singing. He felt terrible that he was ruining the experience for Scott and even worse that he felt angry at God. He had been so sure when she kept appearing in his thoughts and entering his mind that God would re-unite them; he hadn't expected it to end this way.

The music ended and the choir filed off the stage. JD's eyes followed Callie, unable to look away and curious to see who she sat with. She crossed in front of their section and turned down the aisle. JD shifted in his seat to follow her path. A right turn brought her into a row and she took the seat next to . . . *Is that the woman from the inn?*

There was no man beside her, which set off another round of questions. Was he at work or maybe a non-believer who was at home watching football instead? Was there a small chance that maybe there was no man? JD hadn't pegged the fiancé as the type of man ready to settle down and he could certainly imagine the fool fleeing the responsibility of a child.

Though that situation would be worse for Callie, JD couldn't help holding onto the tiny shred of hope that had taken root. However, he was now also tasked with the need to find a new living arrangement soon. He had been so busy the last few days that he hadn't begun looking at apartments yet, but he didn't want to take the chance of running into Callie at the inn either since it appeared the owner was her mother or some other close relative or friend.

Forcing his focus back to the message, JD adjusted his position so that his back was to Callie. He'd have to make an obvious shift to see her now, and that thought kept his eyes on the stage and the thin man with graying hair that was speaking.

*W*hen the service ended, JD glanced back at where Callie had been sitting as he gathered his coat and Bible, but the seats were empty.

Scott turned to follow his gaze. "Are you going to tell me what's going on?"

JD nodded. "Let's grab some lunch and I'll fill you in. Hopefully you can help me with another problem too."

. . .

*M*y hand rubbed my belly as I smiled and waved goodbye to a family with one small rambunctious toddler. Though the little girl was beautiful, I couldn't help but hope that my own daughter would be a little calmer. My mother, no longer much of a singer, had gotten involved in church by joining the greeting committee instead, so each week she either greeted the people coming in or stood at one of the exits to bid those leaving farewell.

I wasn't sure how I had gotten roped into helping today, but I pasted a smile on my face and did my best to ignore the throbbing in my feet. Standing on the stage for the twenty minutes of singing had taken its toll, and I couldn't wait to get home and put my feet up. If only I had someone who would massage them gently as well.

As I scanned the thinning hallway for anyone else headed our direction, two men exiting the front entrance caught my eye. Could it be?

"I'll be right back mom," I called over my shoulder already heading down the carpeted hallway.

The man I could see clearest I didn't recognize. He was tall with short brown hair, but I could have sworn that I'd seen a flash of that chin length brown hair that haunted my dreams. The taller man moved, unhampering my view of the slightly shorter man beside him and my feet stalled. There was no mistaking that face, even though it was only in profile.

Though the hallway traffic had thinned, there were still too many people for me to maneuver through and reach them on time, and besides my feet no longer seemed to want to cooperate. I could yell, but that would be rude in church. Plus, it would attract more attention than I wanted, and on the slim chance that I was wrong, it would be extremely embarrassing. So, for the second time in less than a week, I watched JD walk out of my life again.

With his passage out the door and out of sight, my feet regained their ability to move, and, shoulders sagging, I returned to my mother.

"What was that about?"

"It was him again. I saw JD but I couldn't reach him in time. I have to find him, mother. I just have to."

"So, let me get this straight," Scott said after JD had laid out the whole story, "The girl you thought you loved is pregnant with another man's baby here in this town, and her mother is the owner of the place you're staying?"

"Okay, so I'm not positive it's her mother, but that's the gist of it," JD said. "Why are you smiling?"

"I'm sorry," Scott laughed, "It's just that your story sounds a little like a bad Lifetime movie. My ex-girlfriend used to watch them all the time. I think that might be one reason we broke up."

A small smile tugged at the corners of JD's mouth. It did sound like a bad lifetime movie. He just wished it weren't reality and that it wasn't his current situation. "So, can you help me or not?"

Scott nodded as he finished chewing the bite of burger he had in his mouth. "I can. I have a friend who deals with the residential. I'm sure she can get you a great place quickly."

JD should have felt relieved, but that nagging seed of hope reared its head and reminded him that he didn't know for sure. There had been no man next to her during church, and he hadn't seen a ring, though she had been too far away to see her hand clearly. What if there was a chance she was single and he was leaving the best connection to her? Of course, on the other hand, he couldn't stay there forever anyway. He would need to get an apartment for the rest of his stay regardless of Callie.

"Cindy said she can meet you tomorrow at ten to show you a few places. Are you free then?"

JD glanced up. He had been so absorbed in his own thoughts that he hadn't even seen Scott texting on the phone he held in his hand.

"Yes, I can do that." The image of Callie's raven hair faded from his mind as he forced his mind to focus on Scott. He could deal with the torturous thoughts of her later.

CHAPTER 13

*A*fter a long night with little sleep, JD packed his bags and headed downstairs to let the owner know that today would be his last day.

The woman looked up from the counter as he descended the last step, and JD realized she really did resemble an older version of Callie. She had to be her mother, with the same dark hair and eye shape. Her eyes were more of a hazel color than the emerald green of Callie's but the shape was the same.

"Hello," he said as he approached. "I wanted to let you know that I'll be checking out today."

Her smile faltered as her brow knitted together. "Oh, I'm sorry to hear that. Is there anything we can do to make you want to stay?"

He thought about asking about Callie right then. The words 'Can you set me up with your daughter' jumped into his brain, beating against his throat to come out, but he swallowed them away. The woman would probably think he was a stalker if he uttered them. "No, thank you. It was wonderful, but I'll be staying longer and thought an apartment might be a little more convenient."

The smile returned to her face at the realization that he wasn't dissatisfied with her inn or her service. "I can certainly understand that, though I'm still sorry to see you go." She clicked a few buttons on the computer to her right and a small printer whirred to life, spitting out a single sheet of paper. Picking up the sheet, she glanced over it before sliding it across the countertop to him. "I just need you to fill this out."

JD perused the charges. Nothing seemed out of the ordinary, so he initialed on the lines and signed at the bottom.

"Thank you, Mr. Peterson," she said, picking up the paper. She glanced at the lines and then her eyes widened. "I'm sorry, does this say JD Peterson?" A quiver of excitement laced her voice, and her eyes held the look of a kid at Christmas.

"Yes. I'm JD Peterson."

A smile broke out on her face before she could contain it, but just for a second. A blink of his eyes later and she had composed herself, and only the sparkle in her eyes remained, making him wonder if he had imagined the whole thing.

"And what time will you be leaving tonight? So I can have the cleaning crew do your room," she added hastily.

"I should be ready to vacate by six."

"Six," she repeated, "Wonderful."

JD wondered at her odd behavior, but he had only an hour before he had to meet Cindy and the rumbling in his stomach reminded him that he hadn't eaten, so putting the incident out of his mind, he turned into the quaint dining room to grab some breakfast.

Four small circular tables covered in white tablecloths

filled the room. This morning they were all empty. Everyone else must have already eaten.

Dropping his coat over the back of one of the chairs, he grabbed a plate from the buffet table and filled it with food. He was going to miss this aspect. The woman was an amazing cook, presenting an array of delicious delicacies. This morning there was a green and gold quiche that smelled heavenly, some sort of breakfast casserole that reminded him of campfire meals, and a plate of homemade cinnamon rolls. Since it was his last day, he piled one of each on his plate. Might as well eat his fill.

*M*y phone buzzed again on my desk. Someone was sure insistent; the phone had buzzed at least four times since I had started reading this document, but I knew if I picked it up, I would be distracted and lose my place. When I finished the document, I picked up the phone. Four text messages from my mother filled the screen. Was there an emergency? My mother never texted; she always said she hated the impersonal aspect of it. As I scrolled to the top to read the first message, my hand flew to my mouth.

JD was at the inn? The last message stated that he was checking out and leaving at six. I glanced at my watch. It was almost noon. If I worked through lunch and finished this research, I could leave at four, which would give me a little time to clean up.

The intercom buzzed as I hit the button. "Tina? I need you to order me in some lunch. I'm working straight through today."

. . .

"*I*t doesn't look like much, but it comes furnished. All it really needs is a woman's touch." Cindy leaned against the small bar in the kitchen and flashed a seductive smile.

Instead of answering, JD turned away pretending to consider the place again. All morning she had been dropping suggestive hints, blocking doorways so he had to touch her to walk by, dropping her hand flirtatiously on his arm as she pointed features out in the apartments, and now striking a seductive pose. It wasn't that she wasn't pretty. With her short dark hair and small build, she was nice to look at, but she wasn't Callie.

"I'll take it," he said, partly because it fit the bill he was looking for and partly because he didn't want to see another place with Cindy.

While she drew up the papers, he perused the small apartment one more time. It wasn't anything grand, but it would do for as long as he was here.

The front door opened to a spacious living room with plush beige carpet. A brown recliner and loveseat filled the room facing a medium sized television. The kitchen had a direct view to the living room and was decorated in beiges and tans. The lone hallway led from the living room down to the bathroom and the one bedroom, both large enough for his needs.

Cindy was right that it needed a woman's touch, and he couldn't help picturing Callie hanging pictures or helping him pick out throw pillows.

"All done," she said in her sing-song voice. "Shall we celebrate?"

He did want to celebrate, but not with Cindy. "I can't. I need to get my things from the bed and breakfast I was staying at."

Her full lips formed a perfect pout. He wondered if she practiced the look in the mirror and how many men stumbled over themselves when she flashed it. "Well, another time then," she purred. "You have my number now, and I know where you live."

He tried for a polite smile and shook her hand, hoping she'd pick up on the hint that he wasn't interested. With a final longing look at him, she handed over the keys, gathered her paperwork, and left.

After locking the door to make sure she didn't return, JD collapsed on the loveseat with a sigh. He needed to pick up some food from a grocery store to stock the fridge, but he could afford to rest for a moment. Avoiding Cindy's advances had been quite exhausting.

I sat in the car staring at the front of the inn. My heart was thudding in my chest and my throat felt like the Sahara Desert. In a moment, I would be face to face with JD for the first time in months. Would he still be interested in me now that I was pregnant? Only one way to find out. With a final deep breath, I stepped out of the car.

The wind caught my hair, whipping it about my face. So much for the thirty minutes I had spent making sure every lock was in place.

I shoved my hands deeper in my coat pockets as the chill in the air bit through my layers. Though it was a short walk up the steps, I found myself shivering as I reached for the door handle.

"Callie?"

The timbre of the voice behind me sent a tingle down my spine. I had missed that, the way he said my name.

I turned around slowly. JD stood at the end of the

sidewalk wearing a pair of jeans and a brown leather jacket. The wind tousled his hair as I longed to.

"Hi, JD." I wanted to say more, to sound eloquent, but words failed me yet again.

He took a step toward me, his eyes never leaving my face. "What are you doing here?"

"I could ask you the same thing." Pulling my coat tighter across my belly – I'd explain that to him later – I stepped down to the sidewalk.

"I'm here for work." Another step, only three steps separated them now.

"My mother told me you were here, and I needed to see you before I lost you again." Only two steps remained.

"Why?" One step. "What about Daniel?"

"There is no more Daniel." A small smile tugged at my lips, and I covered the final distance, feeling the heat radiate off his body even as the wind blew against us. "There hasn't been since a few weeks after I returned from the Caribbean." I could reach out and touch him now if I wanted, if I wasn't afraid he might bolt. The emotion in his eyes was unclear, but I hoped he was happy to see me.

His eyes roamed my face, but he said nothing. I couldn't handle the silence. "I found your travel books and the picture when I got home. It sits on my nightstand. I've looked at it every night, wishing I had done things differently there. I should never have taken Daniel back. You were right, and I'm sorry."

As conflicting emotions battled across his face, I wondered why. Was he seeing someone now?

"What about the baby?" he asked.

My eyes widened. "How did you know?" I had picked this coat particularly because it hid my baby bump.

He stared at me; he clearly wasn't answering my question until I answered his.

"I'll tell you all about it, but the father isn't in the picture." The wind found a hole in our electric current and nipped at me; I shivered, wishing he would take me in his arms.

"So, there's no one?"

The small smile broadened as I shook my head. "No one, but you, I hope."

The words were barely out of my mouth before his right hand was in my hair, his left on the small of my back, and his lips on mine. They were everything I had imagined, soft and firm and intense, like he couldn't get enough. The electricity traveled down my body, warming me against the chilly wind.

He pulled back, his eyes wild. "I'm sorry. I didn't mean – "

"Don't be sorry," I said, placing a finger on his lips. "I've wanted you to do that since the day at the falls."

He brought my hand to his chest as he pulled me closer and met my lips again. The kiss was softer this time, slower, but no less full of emotion.

When he pulled back, I could see that he was struggling to catch his breath just as I was. A tingling was still racing through my body, and my heart was beating so fast it was like a drum in my ear.

A slow smile spread across his face. "I've wanted to do that from the moment I saw you."

We stood there at the end of the sidewalk with the wind whipping around us. He held both of my hands in his, and though the temperature was chilly, neither of us felt the cold.

"I have so much to tell you," I finally said, breaking the magic spell for the moment, "but first I have to tell my mother I found you."

"I get the feeling I owe your mother a thank you," he said entwining his fingers with mine.

"I think we both do."

Hand in hand, we walked into the bed and breakfast. My mother stood at the counter but her eyes were trained on the doorway. As we entered, her eyes lit up, and she hurried out from behind the counter.

Her eyes landed on our clasped hands and her smile magnified. "I take it this is the right JD then."

I smiled up at the man I had only dreamed about, still unable to believe he was here next to me. "It is."

"I assume I have you to thank for Callie showing up here," JD said.

She shrugged, "A mother has to do what she can."

"Well, I truly thank you, but if you don't mind, I'm going to steal your daughter to dinner. I'm starving."

With that, he whisked me back outside and into his car. Minutes later, we had parked at a quiet Italian restaurant.

After opening my door, JD took my hand again and led the way inside. The building was small from the outside, but opened impressively inside. Ten tables and a few booths filled the dimly lit room. Candles glowed on every table, and soft light from the ceiling completed the ambiance.

A young woman in a black skirt and starched white shirt greeted us and led us to the farthest booth. There weren't many other patrons in the restaurant, but the booth blocked out most of what little noise there was. It was almost like being in our own private world.

JD reached for my hand again as soon as we sat down, but I didn't mind. My hands felt empty now if they weren't touching his.

"I have so much I want to ask you," JD said. "Tell me what happened since you left the Caribbean."

I took a deep breath. "That's quite a story, but I'll try. When Daniel and I returned from the trip, I started to see parts of his personality I didn't like." My face clouded as I remembered the ultimatum he had issued. "When he found out I was pregnant, he said he didn't want the responsibility of being a parent. He wanted to be free to do what he wanted, so he forced me to choose between him and the baby. I chose the baby."

"He didn't want to raise his own child?"

A heat seared across my face, and I dropped my eyes. I hadn't wanted to tell him so soon, but it was the perfect opportunity "It's not his, but he didn't even know that, and he didn't want to raise the child. I knew I couldn't stay with someone like that." I bit my lip, hoping that my admission of my philandering behavior wouldn't scare him away. I looked up through lowered lids, but JD's face was passive. His hand still caressed mine though.

"The baby's not Daniel's?"

Though I had known he would ask the question, the actual words coming out of his mouth speared my heart. "I had a bad night shortly after Daniel left me. I drank too much with a friend and ended up in the apartment of a guy I met that night. I've never done anything like that before, and I promise it will never happen again." The words spilled out in a rush; I was so afraid that he would get angry and leave before I had a chance to explain.

"Callie, I'm not here to judge you. I've done some things I'm not proud of in my life too."

I wondered what he had done, but he didn't elaborate.

"What matters to me is the father. Does he want the baby? Will he come back in our lives?"

I shook my head slowly. He wasn't angry? I should have known; he was so different. *Wait, did he say 'our' lives?* "I don't think so. I told him about the baby as soon as I knew, and he was not pleased. He signed away his parental rights, so even if he tries to come back, he has no standing."

He nodded, and just like that the discussion was over. I stared at him, my affection deepening.

The waitress appeared with a tray of freshly baked bread and I snatched one before it even had time to cool. I had been so nervous about meeting JD that I hadn't eaten much all day, and my stomach was definitely protesting now.

Across the table, JD's lips pulled into a bemused smile. "Are you going to save some room for dinner?"

A tingling swept up the back of my neck and across my face. I swallowed the bite in my mouth and put the rest of the bread down. "I'm sorry. I didn't eat well today, and I'm eating for two now."

"Don't be sorry. I find it endearing." His voice was soft; his eyes steady on my face.

Though I knew he was sincere, I wasn't used to someone looking at me the way JD was now. My eyes dropped to the table top and the remainder of the bread I hadn't shoved in my mouth.

"I've told you my story. Now tell me more about you. We never talked about what you did while we were in the Caribbean."

JD took a sip of his water glass, "I manage my dad's companies because my dad had a heart attack a few years ago, and he decided to retire to Florida with my mom. We run a few Christian publishing companies. In fact, you should write about your story. I bet it would make a great book."

The thought of sharing my story with complete strangers mortified me. I was still embarrassed by my choices and often felt people were looking at me wondering where my ring was, but the verse about being a prophet pushed to the front of my mind. Could that have been the verse's cryptic meaning? Using my own mistakes to help others from making the same ones? "I'll think about it." I smiled. "So what were you doing in the Caribbean? You said you go there every year."

The waitress interrupted the conversation to take our

order, and then JD continued. "I do. I take brochures and books about Jesus that we've printed that year and distribute them down there. My dad used to do that every year when I was a kid and so I sort of grew up there. Remember Sammy who braided your hair?"

I nodded. What I remembered more than Sammy was the tingle I had felt at JD's touch and the beginning sparks of attraction.

"Well, he also owns the bar I was working in the night we met, and he helps run a local church there that distributes our materials. I guess it's kind of like missionary work, except I only stay there for a couple of weeks. I give him the books and he gives them out to the people."

"Wow, that's nice of your company. So are you opening a publishing branch here?"

He chuckled. It was a deep, lovely sound, coupled with an even lovelier smile. "No, I'm starting a pregnancy crisis center here."

My eyebrows drew together, creating a stream of wrinkles across my forehead and nose. "What does that have to do with publishing?"

"Nothing," JD laughed, "but the need for one's been weighing on my heart, and my father always taught me to listen to my heart's desire because it's from God when it's also based on principles from His word. So, here I am looking into a place to open up a clinic to help pregnant women make the same decision you did."

My eyes widened and I leaned forward, "Sandra will be so excited. She's been praying for a local clinic, and I want to help your clinic. Whatever you need. Well, whatever you need that I can do with a baby on the way," she laughed.

"I think you look even more beautiful with a baby on the way. The glow suits you. While you were stunning then, you don't even look like the same woman I met in the Caribbean."

"I'm not." My gaze dropped to our entwined hands and then back up at him through lowered lids. "You were right. Having a relationship with God changes you."

Before JD could reply, the waitress returned with our plates, setting down a delectable chicken alfredo in front of me and a large plate of lasagna in front of JD. My mouth watered as the aroma wafted up to my nose.

This time, I joined JD when he prayed over dinner. When the prayer ended, I filled my fork with pasta. The creamy alfredo sauce flowed like honey down my throat and before I knew it, my plate was empty. As JD still had half of his lasagna, I reached my fork onto his plate and scooped up a bite.

"Hey, what do you think you're doing?" he asked.

"Helping you out." I smiled and brought the forkful to my mouth. Though I wasn't the biggest lasagna fan, it too was delicious.

JD shook his head, a smile playing at his lips. As I watched him finish eating, I pictured my life with him. An image of the two of us in the kitchen cooking while a small child played at our feet filled my mind. He turned to kiss me before I leaned down to scoop up the child.

"What are you thinking?" JD asked.

His voice shattered my daydream, and a blush spread across my cheeks. I didn't want to tell him about the daydream, not yet at least, not until I knew for sure how he felt. "Nothing," I said. "I just can't remember when I had a nicer dinner."

"Me either."

"What does the JD stand for?" Though I hadn't been curious when we met, I had often wondered over the last few months when I thought about him. This time the question jumped out before I could stop it.

He smiled at the odd request, "Jonathon Daniel."

I blinked at him, sure that I had heard him wrong.

"What is it?" he asked.

"Do you remember the day back in the Caribbean when I told you I prayed?" He nodded, and I continued, "Well, I prayed for God to send Daniel back to me. It appears he answered my prayer, only with a different Daniel than I thought."

"I told you he works in mysterious ways," JD said. His broad smile perfectly matched the feeling coursing through my body."

He finished his plate, and when the bill came, JD picked up the tab. I tried to protest, but he reminded me that I would be taking a pay cut, at least for a while when I went on maternity leave.

The cold hit again as soon as we stepped outside, and I shivered. The sun had set while we ate and the temperature had cooled even more. JD wrapped his arm around my shoulder, pulling me closer to him. I basked in the warmth and security he offered.

He allowed the car to idle a minute, letting the heater warm up. "Shall I take you back to the inn?"

I wanted to say no. I wanted him to come home with me so I could stay wrapped in his arms. An unnatural fear that this was all a dream and I would lose him again had settled on my shoulders, and I longed for his reassurance. "I suppose that would be best," I said instead. I knew he wouldn't have come even if I asked. "I do have work tomorrow, but will you come over after I get off?"

"I'd love to," he said, and the fear abated. I nestled down in the seat, letting my mind wander again, as we drove off.

The inn was close, and too soon, we had arrived. Before

my hand touched the handle, he was out of his side of the car and opening my door. I had never felt more like a princess. His warm hand enveloped mine, pulling me up from the car and to his chest.

His arms wound around my waist, and as if on instinct, my arms encircled his neck.

JD's eyes were bright, full of emotion and unsaid words. My lips parted, and my face turned up to his. An invisible current seemed to run between us, pushing his face closer to mine until our lips met. As the kiss deepened, my hands tightened around his neck, and his arms pressed me tighter against him. I felt molded to his body, a perfect fit.

Though desire was running rampant through my body and it would have been easy to get back in the car and head to my place, I forced myself to sever the kiss. This time was going to be different, but I couldn't help feeling pleased that he was just as breathless as I was.

"Good idea," he said, shaking his head. "I could lose myself with you." He placed a final soft kiss on my lips and then headed to his own car.

I took those words to bed that night. We both had agreed to wait on an intimate relationship, but I couldn't keep my mind from wandering. Clad in my favorite oversized t-shirt, I curled up in bed, imagining JD beside me. I had never felt sexier or more desired. My hand absently rubbed my belly, and Hope moved against it.

"I don't want to jinx it, little one, but I think he could be 'the one.'"

CHAPTER 14

*J*D woke before the alarm the next morning, a smile still on his face. He had slept better last night than he had in ages, and he had Callie to thank for that.

He was whistling as he met Scott for coffee that morning. After their lunch on Sunday, they had agreed to meet once a week for coffee. Scott hadn't said he was ready to accept Jesus, but JD was pleased that he seemed willing to meet and discuss it.

"Well, someone looks like the cat who ate the canary," Scott said as JD slid in the chair across from him.

JD tried to contain the grin on his face, but it was impossible. "You would be too if you'd had the night I did."

Scott's eyes widened under raised eyebrows. "I didn't think that fit in your philosophy."

"No, not that," JD laughed, shaking his head, "though it was the first time in a long time that it was hard to control that urge. No, I ran into Callie."

"The pregnant woman from church?" Scott's face twisted

with confusion. "I guess I'm not seeing why that's a good thing."

"Because," JD said, wiggling his eyebrows, "she's not with the guy anymore."

"Ah, now I see. Good for you, man, that's great." Though Scott's words were positive, there was a wistfulness in his tone.

"Spill it," JD said. He didn't know Scott well, but he could tell something was troubling him.

Scott shrugged. "It's the anniversary of my divorce. I guess it always gets me down a bit. I thought we'd be together forever, you know?"

JD did know. Too many marriages ended in divorce these days, and no one ever came out unscathed. When he married, he hoped his wife would be as committed as he was to making the marriage work, no matter what came their way. An image of Callie walking down the aisle toward him filled his vision, and though he wanted to see it, he pushed it away to focus on Scott.

"Anyway, just ignore me. I'll be fine tomorrow."

JD doubted that, but he hoped that the more Scott came to church with him, the more God would fill the hole in his heart until the woman God had in mind for him came along. He made a promise to keep up his coffee meetings with Scott no matter how busy he got.

JD spent the rest of his day buying office furniture, painting, and getting the electricity and plumbing turned on and switched over to his name. It was tedious work, and he couldn't wait to get a staff hired that could help him.

All of that could wait though, because he had a movie date planned with Callie. He stopped at a local florist for a bouquet of flowers on the way to her house. Bypassing the traditional roses, he asked the woman to make up something special. What she handed him was a veritable feast for the eyes. Roses of several different colors, some blue flower he didn't recognize, a few carnations, and sprigs of baby's breath filled the purple tissue paper. It was perfect, original and special just like Callie.

I bustled around the apartment as quickly as I could given my size; no one had told me how much harder everyday tasks would be when my stomach grew. JD would be here any minute and while I normally kept the place neat, I had been too tired lately to clean when I got off work. Because of that, there were a few papers lying about and several dishes in the sink.

As I put the last dish in the dishwasher, the doorbell rang. Perfect timing. A glance in the hallway mirror as I passed it reassured me, and I threw the door open with a smile.

JD stood on the other side with the most beautiful bouquet of flowers I had ever seen.

"For the prettiest woman I know," he said, holding them out.

"Oh, JD, they're beautiful. Come in." Taking the flowers, I ushered him inside. "Let me just put them in some water."

He followed me into the kitchen and leaned against the counter as I pulled out a vase and filled it with water. Though I tried to keep my focus on the task, my treacherous eyes kept darting to the left to admire the way JD's jeans hugged his form and how the hunter green of his shirt made his eyes a darker shade of green, like a forest at dusk. I didn't think I would ever tire of looking in those eyes.

"There all done." I pushed the flowers into the middle of

the bar, a kind of buffer to quell the tension stirring inside me.

"Good, let's watch a movie. Did you pick one out?"

"I wasn't sure what you liked to watch, so I picked a few. I have a few romantic comedies and an action movie." I led him back to the living room and motioned to the movies spread out on the coffee table.

"You have The Princess Bride? I love this movie." The smile on his face brought out his boyish charm and I laughed.

"Me too. I used to watch it all the time in High School. And then I found the book." The book had become a favorite of mine, and I was a die-hard fan of the movie and could quote nearly every line, but he didn't need to know that.

After inserting the movie, I joined him on the couch. He opened up his arm, and I accepted the invitation, nestling myself in the crook. His hand began to trace slow circles on my shoulder, sending tingles all the way down to my toes. Snuggling closer, I laid my hand against his chest. The urge to unbutton his shirt and feel his chiseled chest first hand flitted through my body, but I pushed it aside. No matter how hard it was, I was going to do this relationship God's way. Besides, there was a comfort in just being held and inhaling the masculine scent that JD exuded. It had been months since I'd had that.

I turned my face to look up at him. His skin was still the same bronze color I remembered, but a light stubble dotted his face this time that hadn't been there before. He caught me looking at him and lifted my chin before lowering his lips to mine. Heat flooded through me, and my heart thudded in my chest. This time he was the one to pull back, and though I didn't want the kiss to end, I was grateful he had done it.

All of my plans to go slow seemed to fly from my mind when he kissed me.

He smiled and brushed a strand of hair from my face. I could get used to his touch and the way he looked at me, like I was the most valuable item in the world. Daniel had never looked at me like that. He had desired me sure, but not with the same respect that JD did. I understood now what Sandra had meant when she said a Godfearing man wouldn't want to do anything to cause you to sin. I could tell that JD desired me in the same way Daniel had, but he was going to do it right, as God had intended. I just hoped I would be able to remain as strong.

CHAPTER 15

*J*D's fingers touched the black velvet box in his pocket. He had picked it up on his way to meeting Scott for coffee, and he'd been unable to keep his fingers from touching it.

"Okay, what's going on, man?" Scott snapped his fingers in front of JD's face. "You haven't heard one word I said."

JD blinked, bringing his focus back to the present. He wanted to tell Scott his news; heck he wanted to shout it from the rooftops, but he also knew Scott was battling a feeling of loneliness, and he didn't want to rub it in.

"Spill it." Scott leaned back and crossed his arms.

JD withdrew his hand from his pocket and held out the black box. "Before you say anything, I know it's fast, but I've known I loved Callie for months, and I don't want to take the chance of losing her again."

Scott opened the box and let out a low whistle. "It's exquisite, so what's the problem?"

A sigh escaped JD's lips as he thought back over the last week. Callie had been home late every night, and while she usually called to let him know, he still wasn't enjoying eating dinner alone. He'd had enough of that to last a lifetime. "It's her job. She's been working long hours, and while I want to propose, I don't want to marry someone who will be gone most evenings, you know?"

Scott closed the box and handed it back. "As you know, I'm no expert, but I'd say talk to her. If she knew how you felt, maybe she'd decide to make a change."

JD nodded. Scott was right. He'd talk to her tonight, and if all went well, then he could propose. He didn't want to think about what he'd do if all didn't go well.

I groaned as I glanced at my watch. I was going to be late again. This latest case had me working nearly twelve hour days, and I'd had to cancel on JD twice already this week. He'd said he had something important to talk about, so I could only hope that he'd forgive me.

Grabbing my purse as soon as the car was parked, I hurried up to his door and knocked.

It opened a moment later, but JD's face was not smiling. "Come on in."

He held the door open, and I bit my lip as I stepped inside. He wasn't going to break up with me, was he? I knew this week had been hard on him, but I'd thought he was the type to stick it out.

"Sit down." He pointed to the couch, and a feeling of dread blanketed me. "Callie, I love you. I'm pretty sure I've loved you from the moment I saw you, but I'm not loving your job right now."

I nodded. "I know. It is busy this week, but when this case is over, it will get better."

"What about when the next case comes along?"

"I . . . what do you want me to do, quit my job?" Anger stirred in my stomach.

"I was wondering if you would come work for me. The hours will be better, and I need someone to help with hiring the staff and putting the final touches on the office."

I considered his proposal. Once, I had thought of nothing other than being a lawyer, but the hours were taking their toll on me, and I knew it would be worse once Hope arrived.

"I could offer you a generous benefit package with maternity leave. Plus, it would be amazing to work with my wife every day."

My head popped up. *Did he say wife?*

JD pulled a black box from his pocket and opened the lid.

My breath caught in my throat, and tears of joy pricked my eyes. I looked from him down to the quarter carat diamond ring sparkling in his hands, and nodded.

He slipped the ring out of the box and onto my finger. The light caught the stone, sending arcs of color on the wall. It was the most stunning ring I had ever seen. "Yes," I said, "to both your questions."

"I know it's getting closer to your due date," he said, "but I wanted us to at least be engaged before Hope comes. Then we can have the wedding after, when you are up for it."

I shook my head. "No, I want to do it before. We can do a small service at the church. I'm sure Pastor Tony would marry us."

"Callie, are you sure? We've got the opening of the center coming soon, and we still need to get your apartment ready for Hope –

"I'm sure," I said, cutting him off. "I want Hope to be officially yours before she's born."

He smiled. "Okay, we'll ask Pastor Tony tomorrow."

. . .

I looked around the office I had called my second home for the last few years. Though I had often thought I would be leaving this place, I had always assumed it would be for a bigger office, not a completely different career.

I wasn't sad though. The long hours had taken their toll on my pregnant body, and I was looking forward to getting off earlier. Plus, my priorities had shifted. I no longer longed to be partner; now I just wanted to have time to spend with my daughter and my fiancé. Fiancé. I still hadn't totally wrapped my head around that, but the ring on my finger served as a constant reminder.

Hopefully, there would be no hitches in the wedding planning. Getting married eight months pregnant hadn't been in my dream wedding, but I knew I loved JD, and I wanted both of our names to be on the birth certificate when Hope arrived. That was now more important than a fancy wedding or even wearing the perfect dress. I just hoped we could get it all planned in three weeks' time.

"I'm going to miss you," Tina said, sniffling back tears as I approached her desk. In my hands was a small box with my few personal items packed.

"I'll miss you too, but I'll still be in the city. We'll get together. Plus, I'll see you at the wedding." Of all the things I would miss about my job, Tina was at the top of the list. I gave her a final hug, waved goodbye to everyone else, and walked out of the building.

A mixture of fear and relief washed over me as I climbed in the car. I was excited to be helping JD out at the center, but a worry persisted that I would miss being a lawyer. The last thing I wanted to do was resent leaving. "Lord, please send me your peace." A calmness covered my shoulders and warmed my body, and I eased the car into drive to meet JD at the center.

When I arrived, he ushered me in, planting a quick kiss on my lips and leaving me wanting more. The smell of new carpet and wet paint permeated the air.

"I'm so glad you're here. I set up interviews for today, and I'd really like your input."

I glanced around the nearly finished office space, surprised at how close he was to being able to open. Not only were the new carpets laid and the walls repainted, but the receptionist's desk was installed and the waiting chairs were stacked in one corner of the room.

"So, the doctors have already been hired, but we need to hire three nurses, a book keeper, and a receptionist," JD said, rifling through a stack of papers.

I had hoped the afternoon would be a little more relaxing, but wanting to help JD out in any way I could, I followed him into one of the offices that had also been finished. He had set up a table and a few chairs.

"Make yourself comfortable here, and I'll get you some tea. You won't have to move an inch. I'll bring the interviewees back to you."

I smiled up at him. As my due date got closer, he grew more and more attentive and doting. He had even left his own apartment and driven to the store at midnight the other night to buy me nachos and pickles, which he had dropped off with a quick kiss before returning to his own place.

Minutes later, he returned with a steaming mug of green tea for me, and the parade of interviewees began.

When the last one was gone, we discussed the merits of each, agreeing nearly completely on our favorites.

"How much longer do you think the center needs before it opens?" I asked as he gathered up the resumes.

"Honestly? I think we can open in two weeks just before

the wedding. I think Rebekah will be able to handle a few days without me at the very beginning."

An elaborate honeymoon was out of the question for us as I was now too pregnant even to fly safely, but I didn't mind. To me, the honeymoon would just get to be spending the night curled up in JD's arms. I was growing tired of having to say goodbye to him every night and climb into my bed alone.

"What are you thinking about?" JD asked, wrapping his arms around me. Due to my ever-increasing belly, they no longer completely encircled me but landed on the back of my hips.

My lips pulled into a seductive smile as I wound my arms around his neck. "I was thinking that the perfect honeymoon will just be the day I don't have to say goodnight to you and I can wake up with you beside me the next morning."

His lips parted as his eyes filled with desire. "I can't wait for that day either."

My nerve endings tingled as his mouth closed on mine. A heat flared inside as his tongue explored my mouth. His lips then traveled down my neck, landing on the soft flesh between my collar bone and my neck. My breath caught in my throat, and my hands twisted in his hair. If he could affect me this deeply with all our clothes on, I could only imagine the havoc he could wreak with no barrier between us.

With the wedding quickly approaching, the last thing on my to-do list had been the nursery. I had been pushing it off, due to work, but now that I had some time, it had jumped to number one on the list. The last thing I wanted was for this baby to arrive and have no nursery.

JD had agreed to take the afternoon off and shop with me, and both Scott and Lexi had agreed to help us finish that evening. Lexi's acceptance had surprised me as she had distanced herself after the few times she had come to church with me, but evidently Lexi had a soft spot for babies.

"*L*avender? Are you sure?" JD raised his eyebrows as we stood in the paint aisle debating on colors to paint Hope's room.

"She's a girl, silly." I laughed and swatted him playfully. "She is going to love pinks and purples."

"I guess I'm going to have to get used to all this girly stuff." He smiled as he picked up three cans of paint and put them in the cart.

"If you plan on sticking around you are."

We grabbed some paint brushes and tape and then headed to the baby aisle of the store where I picked out a white crib and changing table, a cream-colored rocker, and a small white dresser. JD muscled them all in the cart and followed me as I turned to the clothing aisle.

My final paycheck hadn't been extraordinary, but the office had pooled together money to present as a wedding/baby gift, and it had been enough to cover most of what I needed to purchase.

Scott's car was in the parking lot when we returned to the apartment, and he hurried over to help JD unload the paint and the heavier nursery furniture we had purchased. Lexi showed up as I was returning for a second time to get all the bags of clothes out of the car.

"These are so cute." Lexi said a she held up a tiny pair of purple jammies dotted with white butterflies.

JD and Scott had taken over Hope's room to paint and assemble furniture, so Lexi and I were sorting clothes in the living room. I was relieved as the couch was much more comfortable to sit in lately.

I smiled and folded a pink onesie. "Makes you think about having one of your own one day, doesn't it?"

"Not until I find a good man like JD."

Pulling a blanket out of the bag, I snipped the tag off. "Well, if you'd come back to church with us, I'm sure God would help you find one."

Lexi bit her lip and pulled out another outfit. "I know; maybe this week."

I changed the subject so as not to make Lexi uncomfortable, but I continued to pray for her as we worked. When we were done sorting, I ordered a pizza and then we turned on the TV to pass time until the men were finished.

Half an hour later, Scott and JD emerged, sporting a few purple spots and a bit more sweat.

"Perfect timing." I pushed myself off the couch and wrapped my arms around JD, placing a quick kiss on his lips. "The pizza just got here."

JD led us all in prayer as we gathered around the table. "Lord, thank you for this food and for the amazing friends you have brought us. Bless them and bless this house and help us to remember the great sacrifice you gave for us and to never waste a day doing what does not honor you. Amen"

"Amen." As soon as the prayer was finished, I snatched a piece of pizza. For some reason tonight, I was craving cheese. I almost had the slice to my mouth when Scott cleared his throat and began to speak. I stared longingly at the slice, but put it down to give him my full attention.

"I want to say something." Scott adjusted his shoulders. "You two have been such an amazing example for me. I've been thinking about it for a while, but tonight after painting Hope's room and hearing your prayer, I've decided it's time. I'd like to have a personal relationship with Jesus."

"That's wonderful," JD and I shouted simultaneously. A burst of adrenaline shot through me, masking the hunger for the moment.

"I'm not sure exactly what to do though." Scott swallowed and tapped his hands on the table.

JD touched his arm. "I don't think there's a perfect way, but I can tell you the one we use on our pamphlets. As long as you mean these words, God will accept you: Lord, I know that I'm a sinner and I now believe that you sent your son Jesus to die for me. I believe in and want to trust Him as my Lord and Savior. Please Jesus, come into my heart and lead me. Amen"

Scott repeated the words and tears filled his eyes. "Thank you," he said, wiping his eyes as he finished. "I can't believe I waited so long. I feel like a huge weight has been lifted.

"You're welcome, Brother." JD clapped his arm. "I'm so happy to have you in the family."

I smiled at JD and sneaked a peek at Lexi, who appeared to be lost in thought. *I hope she's thinking about accepting Jesus, too.*

After dinner, Scott and Lexi said their goodbyes and as soon as they had left, JD grabbed my hand. "Okay, now come see the room."

"I'm coming, I'm coming." His excitement was contagious, and I smiled as he led the way down the hall.

Outside Hope's door, he stopped and turned to me. "Eyes closed."

I closed my eyes, and JD's hands covered them. He stood behind me and walked me into the room before dropping his hands. I gasped. The furniture wasn't against the walls yet, as they were still drying, but the white crib had been set up and decorated with the purple and white heart sheets we had bought. The rocker sat a little to the side, and the dresser and changing table finished the look.

"It's beautiful." I couldn't have imagined a more perfect room if I had tried.

JD smiled and wrapped his arms around me. "You're beautiful."

That night, after JD had left to go back to his place, I sat in the rocking chair, rubbing my belly. "This is your room, Hope. I hope you love purple as much as I do." Hope kicked against my hand, bringing another smile to my face. "I may not have done in it the right order, but in just a few days, JD and I will get married. I think he will make an amazing father." Another kick told me that Hope agreed.

❀

Two days before the wedding, the center's grand opening arrived.

JD and I stood inside the center looking around at the finished product. "It's so amazing." I squeezed JD's hand. The main office was warm and inviting with a soft mauve color on the walls and carpet. Comfy chairs and even a few rockers filled the waiting room, and on the end table were packets from nearby adoption agencies and churches. The exam rooms had each been painted a different color and decorated in childlike themes to entertain any children that might come with mothers. We had hired a wonderful staff of Christian men and women, and I couldn't have been prouder of JD.

"Come on, we better get outside before they come looking for us." I followed him to the back exit where we pushed open the rear door and snuck around to join the crowd in the front of the building.

Thankfully, the weather had smiled upon us today. Though still chilly, it wasn't raining, and the crowd looked warm enough in their coats and scarves. Scott waved as we rounded the corner and jogged to meet us. "There you are." He handed JD a pair of scissors. "The people are getting restless, my friend."

JD took the scissors and stepped onto a nearby bench to be seen as he addressed the crowd. "Welcome everyone; we're so pleased to open Faith Pregnancy Center and be able to give women quality care and alternative choices to abortion." Applause erupted from the crowd. "Please feel free to take a tour and take a business card to share it with a friend." He cut the giant red ribbon that stretched across the front door, and the crowd cheered.

As the people began to file inside, a pain flared in my side and I sucked in a breath.

"Are you alright?" There was a thread of fear in his voice that sent tremors through my body.

"I think so." I rubbed my side, trying to convince myself that the pain hadn't been that bad. "Maybe just Braxton Hicks contractions." I wasn't due for another month, so I doubted it was real labor. I wasn't sure if Braxton-Hicks started that early, but it was the most plausible explanation I could come up with.

The tendons in his neck strained against the skin as his eyes traveled my body.

"I'm sure it's just stress from being so worn out." I hoped I sounded reassuring; I didn't want to ruin his big day. "I'll probably be fine if I just go lie down."

"Are you sure?"

"I'm sure. I feel better already. I bet I'll be right as rain tomorrow."

I hugged him goodbye, trying not to grimace as another pain laced my side, and then waddled to my car. Though I hoped it was nothing, a harbinger of dread fluttered at the back of my mind.

CHAPTER 16

*I*gnoring the pain licking up my side, I stepped into my wedding dress. Though the pain had gotten better after I had rested, it hadn't gone away completely, and I had felt the pangs several times the following day as well.

It had taken all my energy to keep my face from showing the pain, but I had kept the information to myself because I didn't want anything to ruin the wedding.

My mother zipped up the dress and smiled at me in the mirror over my shoulder. "I know this isn't the wedding you dreamed of, but I think it will be the marriage you desired."

She was right. As a little girl, I had always dreamed of the perfect dress – some big designer name – and a big wedding, but I'd almost had that with Daniel, and it hadn't turned out well. As I gazed at my reflection, I realized my dreams had also changed.

Even if I hadn't been nearly nine months pregnant, I would have opted for a simple dress similar to the one that hugged my frame and a small, intimate gathering like the crowd waiting in the sanctuary. In fact, other than the pangs in my side, it was nearly the perfect day.

"I think you're right, mom. I can't imagine a man better than JD." As the words left my mouth, tiny black flecks dotted my vision, and I shook my head to clear them.

Worry etched itself on my mother's face. "Are you alright?"

"Yeah, I think I just need to sit down for a minute."

She led me to one of the chairs in the room and helped me sit down. I forced a smile, hoping to ease the lines on my mother's face. "Can you get me some water, mom?"

Her eyes bore into mine, as if trying to decide if she could leave me alone. With a lingering glance, she nodded and exited the room.

Exhaling, I dropped my head back. The pain was getting worse, and now with the black dots, I knew something was wrong. If I could make it through the ceremony, I'd have JD drive me straight to the hospital afterwards, but I had to make it through the ceremony first. *Lord, please help me get through the ceremony.*

A few calming breaths, while my hands rubbed rhythmic circles across my belly, helped ease the pain, and when my mother returned with the water, I felt better.

Lexi and Tina filed in behind my mother, looking beautiful in their rose-pink dresses. JD had picked Scott as his best man, and because he wasn't close to anyone else here yet, he had asked Tina's husband to be the second groomsman.

"It's almost time; are you ready?" Lexi bounced from one foot to the other, barely able to contain her excitement. Her blond hair was pulled up on her head with just a few tendrils hanging down.

"More importantly, are you feeling better?" my mother asked.

"Better? What's wrong?" Tina stepped forward, assuming her own mothering role.

"Nothing, I just felt a little dizzy is all."

Tina's stare now mirrored my mother's. Only Lexi, who had never been pregnant, seemed oblivious to the mood in the room.

"I'm fine, really." I pushed myself up, determined not to grimace or pass out. The little spots still swam in my vision, but I blinked them away.

"Callie, maybe you should get checked out first – "

"No." I interrupted Tina more forcefully than I meant to. "I mean, I will, but after the ceremony, please?"

My pleading eyes must have convinced them because Tina and my mother sighed but agreed. Lexi handed me my bouquet, and we headed down the hallway.

As my father was no longer in the picture, I had asked my mother to walk me down the aisle. Scott and Gary, Tina's husband, met us outside the sanctuary doors, looking dapper in their dress jackets and soft pink ties.

"You look beautiful, Callie," Scott said, and Gary nodded his agreement, though his eyes were focused on his wife.

The music began and we all took a collective breath.

Gary held out his arm, and Tina slipped hers inside, flashing one more worried smile at me before opening the door and beginning her walk down the aisle.

Scott held out his arm to Lexi, who smiled and flashed me a wink.

As the doors closed behind them, I turned to my mother. "Thank you, mom, for always sticking with me and for continuing to pray for me even when I didn't want it."

My mother sniffed and wiped away the tear that had escaped from her eye. "Of course, dear, that's is what mothers do. I'm sure you will do the same for Hope."

Hope fluttered at the mention of her name, and I placed a hand on my stomach to calm her. Another wave of dizziness washed over me, and I closed my eyes briefly, hoping my mother wouldn't notice.

The music started, and my mother held the door open. I searched for JD and his calming presence. If I could just make it down to the end of the aisle.

Glad for my mother's arm that lent extra strength, I focused on putting one foot in front of the other. The black dots were returning, making it difficult to keep my eyes locked on JD, but my feet kept moving, and I made it to JD's side. He took my arm, and I sensed the concern in his eyes.

Forcing a tight smile though the pain was now licking at my lower back almost constantly, I took the last few steps to stand before Pastor Tony with him.

"Dearly beloved," Pastor Tony started, "We are gathered here today to celebrate this man and this woman and their union with and before God. The marriage of one man to one woman is sacred to God. He designed us not to be alone, but to share our life with someone. JD and Callie found each other and have decided to share the rest of their life together. They have written vows they would now like to share with you. JD?"

JD took my hand and stared into my eyes. "Callie, I've loved you from the moment I first met you. Even after we lost touch the first time, I never stopped thinking about you, and I prayed that we would meet again. I thought when you came into my life again it was the happiest day of my life, but I was wrong. This is the happiest day of my life, being here with you and all our friends, and I promise to love you and only you, for as long as we both shall live." He reached behind him and picked up the ring Scott held out, placing it back on my hand – its rightful place.

Gazing at JD, I smiled, and summoning all the strength I could to make my voice even and clear, I repeated the words I had memorized a few days ago. "JD, I met you at one of my lowest points in life, and you saw me at my worst and still cared about me. You taught me about God's love, even though I didn't believe you at first, but you never gave up on me. I knew when we crossed paths again that I loved you, and I promise to love only you and never give up on you as long as we both live." Scott brought the pillow to me, and I slid the ring I had picked for JD onto his finger.

"Jonathon Daniel Peterson," Pastor Tony began again, "do you take Callie Marie Green as your wife to have and to hold, to love and to cherish, forsaking all others till death do you part?"

"I do."

JD's hands holding mine sent strength down my arms.

"Callie Marie Green, do you take Jonathon Daniel Peterson as your husband to have to hold, to love and to cherish, forsaking all others till death do you part?"

"I do." The word came out barely more than a whisper as another stream of pain coursed up my back and exploded in my head.

"Then by the honor vested in me by the great state of Texas and the Lord above, I now pronounce you husband and wife. You may kiss the bride."

JD wrapped his arms around me and placed his lips to mine. I could hear the crowd clapping, but the pounding in my head overshadowed it, and I sagged against his strong arms.

"Callie, what's wrong?" JD's voice, full of fear, cut through the noise in my head just briefly.

"I think . . . I need . . ." I gasped and then slipped out of his grasp and fell to the floor. The pain that was happening now couldn't be Braxton Hicks. It licked up my left side, and the spots returned with a vengeance, dancing intricate maneuvers in my vision. A pounding in my head stirred nausea causing me to grab my stomach.

A collective gasp rippled through the audience followed by a hushed murmur. The people on stage all dropped to my side.

"Someone call 911."

JD brushed my hair back and cradled my head. I concentrated on breathing and whispering a prayer that Hope was okay. I hadn't fallen directly on my side, but I knew any fall while pregnant could be bad.

Moments later, two EMTs rushed in, carrying a stretcher.

"Can you tell us your name, ma'am?"

"Callie Green, no sorry, Peterson." I smiled up at JD as the paramedic took my blood pressure and shined something in my eye.

"So, Callie, what happened here?"

The paramedic's blond face appeared again. She appeared close to my age.

"I've been having some pain and spots in my vision."

"Spots? You didn't mention spots," my mother said. Her voice was a mixture of fear and admonishment.

"Sorry, they come and go, but after the headache, they got pretty bad, and I think that's when I collapsed."

"There's a headache now too?" Tina's concerned voice joined in.

"Well, I think you should have come in earlier," the paramedic said, "but you've earned yourself a trip to the hospital."

"At least we're married now, right, Pastor Tony?"

"Don't worry, Callie, it's official. I have the paper right here."

"Oh good, I made it through the ceremony."

The EMT's rolled me onto the stiff board and strapped my arms, legs, and head down. I tried not to focus on all the terrified faces above me. I hadn't meant to scare everyone.

"I'm coming with her," JD said to the paramedics as they began to haul her down the aisle.

"Just one in the ambulance," the blond said. "The others will have to drive themselves."

"We can take the church van. I'll drive."

The inside of the ambulance was bright and silver. A too bright light above my face kept my eyes blinking. JD's face came into view for a moment as he climbed in and then disappeared as he sat down, but I could feel his hand holding mine.

The other EMT, also a woman, but with dark hair pulled back in a severe ponytail, hovered over my face attaching and buckling things I couldn't see. She didn't talk much, and I wished the blond were back here instead. She seemed calmer.

My eyes closed as the ambulance roared to life and the siren began to wail. The sound was too loud, but I had no way to cover my ears with my arms strapped to my side. Instead, I focused on sending words to heaven. Words of supplication in hopes of healing and relief.

When the ambulance stopped, the back doors flew open and the gurney was pulled down. I was now on a bed with wheels, and the world began to whiz by as the hospital doors opened.

The EMTs rattled off my name and age and then some medical jargon I did not comprehend.

A doctor with kind blue eyes appeared, older looking, but maybe that was from the stress of the job. His dark hair was streaked with grey. "Hi, Callie. I'm Dr. Rhodes. We're going to take good care of you."

I smiled and then the pain flared again, and the world went dark.

When my eyes opened again, I was no longer on the hard gurney, but a softer hospital bed instead. My wedding dress had been replaced with a faded blue hospital gown. I hoped they hadn't had to cut it off. An IV tube ran from my left arm to a silver rod holding a clear liquid bag. Some sort of monitoring device was attached to my pointer finger, and there was some weird belt around my belly. A steady beeping and the sound of something scratching on paper filled the room.

There was a small couch and a few chairs in the room, but they were empty. Where had everyone gone?

A moment later, the door opened and JD entered carrying a tray of food. "Oh, thank goodness you're awake," he said, rushing to my side. He set the tray on a side table and leaned over to kiss me.

"How long have I been out?"

"A few hours. The doctors ran some tests, and we're waiting on the results, but they think you passed out from the pain. How is the pain now?"

I took a deep breath and closed my eyes, searching for the pain, but couldn't feel any. "I don't feel any now."

"They gave you some pain killer," he said. "It must be helping."

"Where is everyone else?"

"In the lobby. They're only allowing me until they figure out what's wrong with you."

The door opened again, and Dr. Rhodes entered, carrying a clipboard. "Ah, good, you're awake. How are you feeling?"

"Good for now. Did you find out what's wrong with me?"

His smile straightened, and his face grew serious. "Yes, we did. You have a bad case of preeclampsia. The pain in both your side and your head as well as the vision spots are tell-tale signs, plus your blood pressure is extremely high."

A knife of fear inserted itself and began to twist. "What does that mean?"

"Well, in some cases it would mean that we keep you here and monitor you, but in your case, I fear a seizure. I want to deliver the baby right away."

"But, but she's not forty weeks yet."

He nodded. "I know, she's only thirty-five weeks, but Callie, if we wait and you have a seizure, it could cause you lasting damage."

"Will she be okay at thirty-five weeks? Is she fully developed?"

"Her lungs may still be weak. We'll give you some steroids to help develop her lungs, and I'll schedule a C-section for two days from now. That will give her lungs time to develop. We'll also start you on some anti-seizure medication, but I have to warn you that while it's generally effective, seizures can still happen. The sooner we deliver, the better your chances."

I nodded, trying to abate the fear running rampant through me now, not only for myself but for my daughter. There was one more thing I needed to know though. "Did I . . . did I make it worse by not coming in at the first sign?"

Dr. Rhodes shook his head. "It's hard to say. Your blood pressure might have been a little lower then and we might have been able to get you on medication sooner, but you still probably would have been confined to hospital bed rest so we could monitor you. If you had had a seizure during that time, then yes it would have been worse, but since you didn't, my guess is that the two days didn't make much difference."

Relief flooded my veins and weakened the dam that had been holding back the tears threatening to spill down my cheeks.

"But," he continued, "the next time you have symptoms like that, don't wait, okay?"

Emotion constricted my throat, choking off words, so I nodded. As the doctor left the room, the dam exploded, and a sob escaped. My shoulders began to shake as more sobs wracked my body, and the tears flowed freely.

"Hey, it's okay," JD said, his hand caressing my hair. He leaned down and kissed my forehead, sending waves of comfort over me.

"I'm so sorry. I felt like something bad was going to happen, and I wanted to make sure that you were Hope's legal guardian if anything happened to me."

His green eyes clouded with emotion. "Callie, we could have figured something else out. Please don't keep me in the dark like that again."

"I promise."

**

As he watched her eyes close, his thoughts returned to a time years before with Alexa. She too hadn't told him when she had first gotten sick, and by the time she did, he could nothing but hold her hand and watch her die. He couldn't bear to do that again. When he was sure Callie was asleep again, he stood and stretched. He needed to update everyone in the hall.

He opened the door as quietly as he could and found Dr. Rhodes waiting for him on the other side. "I'm glad I caught you. I need a word."

His words were solemn and heavy like a lead balloon. Fear gripped JD, its icy talons shooting down his shoulders. His knees buckled and he stumbled back, sagging against the wall. "How bad is it?" The words felt like fire in his mouth.

"Worse than I let on," Dr. Rhodes said, "but I needed to calm her down. Stress will only make it worse. She needs to deliver, but in her condition, the risks are much higher."

"What can we do?"

"Unfortunately, not much. We have to let the steroids take effect or we risk losing the baby, but the longer we wait, the more we risk losing Callie. If you're a religious man, I'd say pray."

JD felt like he'd been sucker punched in the gut. He couldn't lose Callie, not after finally finding her and making her his wife. He thanked the doctor, took another moment to compose himself, and then continued to the waiting room. A voice inside told him not to tell everyone the news the doctor had just shared. He needed them to be positive for Callie. For now, only Scott and Pastor Tony would be informed. Perhaps they could help him figure out what to do next.

Every head looked up when JD entered. He hadn't expected so many, but nearly everyone from the wedding was there, along with several members of the church.

"Callie's sleeping right now, but when she wakes, we can take turns visiting her. She has preeclampsia so they want her to stay positive and avoid stress. They are giving her steroids to help develop Hope's lungs, and then they'll perform a C-section. It would be amazing if you all could be praying for peace and for her safety.

As the group began to pair up and bow their heads, JD approached Melanie whose skin had paled. Her hand covered her mouth, and he could tell she was holding back tears. "Will you go sit with her? I need to talk to Tony, and I'd like someone there with her in case she wakes up."

Melanie's eyes bore into his own. "What aren't you telling me?"

"I promise I'll tell you later, but for now, will you trust me?"

It took another long look, but finally she stood and walked toward Callie's room. JD moved on to Scott and motioned for Tony to join them. The three stepped to the far corner, out of hearing range of the others in the room.

"It's not good," JD said. "I'm not sure what else to do, but the doctor said to pray."

"Of course; I'll get Sandra right on calling our members." Tony said. "I'll also call the other pastors I know and spread the word to their prayer teams."

"What can I do?" Scott asked.

"I'll be in the room most of the time," JD said. "Can you relay information to people here or wherever they're gathered?"

Scott nodded in agreement, and Pastor Tony led the three of them in prayer for Callie and Hope.

*C*allie was still sleeping when JD returned to the room. Melanie rose and crossed to him. The questions still brimmed in her eyes, but JD couldn't tell her yet.

"Melanie, can you go to Callie's apartment and get some things?" He thought for a moment of all they might need. "The diaper bag, for one. It's packed and in Hope's room. Maybe some clothes for Callie for if, I mean when," he corrected himself, "she comes home. Toothbrush, toothpaste, oh and her Bible, I know she'll want that."

"Okay." Melanie agreed, and though he could tell she wanted more details, she didn't ask and JD was grateful.

He sat in the chair Melanie had scooted close to the bed and grasped Callie's hand. His eyes closed against the emotions battering to be released and he sent up another stream of prayers. He hated feeling helpless, but he knew that the only thing he could do was to pray for Callie, unceasingly.

CHAPTER 17

*T*he two days that followed were the longest of my life. Though the doctor kept making assurances that the time I had waited hadn't made much of a difference, I still battled a massive guilt every time I thought about it, and I worried about Hope constantly.

On top of that, the monitor on my belly to track Hope's heartbeat wasn't very comfortable, and if I moved too far in either direction, the sensors would lose track of Hope's heartbeat and nurses would rush in to check on me, so I couldn't get decent rest. I had to lie almost completely on my back, and it had gone numb sometime yesterday. And as they would only let me out of bed to go to the bathroom, I couldn't stretch or take a shower, which left me feeling sore and grimy.

To top it all off, the doctors didn't want me overstimulated or stressed out, so they capped the visitors to two at a time. Because there were so many people wanting to visit, this meant an almost constant flow of people coming in and out, at least until I got too tired and had to take a nap.

Still, I would gladly relive the past two days over again if it could mean foregoing the C-section today. Though I knew the hospital staff did them every day, one hadn't been in my plan, and as much as I was trying to give everything to God, there were some things I just couldn't let go.

As the nurses came into the room, my breath stopped. The fear I had been pushing away filled my body, and my veins ran ice cold. Unable to speak, I squeezed JD's hand and shot him a look.

JD turned to the nurses. "Can you give us a minute?"

The team left and JD, my mother, and I joined hands. "Lord, I don't know what your purpose is with this event in Callie's life, and we want your will to be done, but we ask that you keep Hope and Callie safe and bring them both back to us after this is over. Give us peace with whatever happens and courage to keep doing your will. Amen." His eyes perused my face, and he squeezed my hand and swallowed several times before he could continue speaking. "I love you Callie, and whatever happens, I will be right here with you."

I could see the sheen in his eyes, and I nodded, trying to contain my own emotion to keep my tears from flowing again. "I love you too," I whispered, hoping it wouldn't be the last time I said it.

My mother leaned down and placed a kiss on my forehead. She was unable to stop the tears flowing down her face. "I love you precious girl, and whatever happens, I am so proud of you."

The door opened and one of the nurses poked her head back in. "I'm sorry, but we really need to go now; the room is ready and the anesthesiologist is waiting." She entered as well as three other nurses. JD and my mother stepped back as the nurses unlocked the bed and wheeled me and my IV out into the hallway.

Usually, JD would have been able to accompany me into

a C-section delivery, but the doctors were sure that my case was so advanced that I might need immediate medical attention, so he was not admitted. This information did nothing to calm the ball of nerves in my stomach.

As the bed was wheeled down the hall, I took deep breaths to calm my nerves. Lights flashed overhead, and I closed my eyes to avoid the nausea. I pictured the field of daisies from my dream so long ago and the little blond angel who had visited. It didn't stop my heartbeat from reverberating in my ears.

Suddenly, I shivered. The temperature had dropped, and I lost my hold on the daisies. A cold silver, sterile operating room surrounded me as my eyes opened. A bright light hung from the ceiling, and I blinked. Several doctors were already busy prepping in the room. One was sitting on a stool near the bed.

"Hi, I'm Michael," he said, taking my hand. "I have some music. Would you like music during the procedure?"

I didn't know him; I could barely even tell what he looked like with the mask covering the lower part of his face and his hair hidden under a blue cap that matched his scrubs, but his hand sent a wave of comfort nonetheless.

"Do you have any Toby Mac?" My voice sounded small and distorted.

He smiled and squeezed my hand. "You bet. Now, my job is to make sure you aren't feeling any pain so once we numb you, you're going to focus on me and let me know if you feel anything okay?"

I nodded. Michael and a few other doctors helped me onto the operating bed, and then Michael picked up a long needle and injected my back. I grimaced at the pain. It took a few minutes, but as they laid me back, my legs grew numb.

"Okay, can you feel this?" Michael touched a spot on my leg.

I shook my head. I could see him poking my leg, but I could feel nothing.

"How about this?" He touched a different spot.

Again, I shook my head.

"Okay, then I believe we're ready. Let me turn your music on."

I tried to focus on the music instead of the pounding of my heart. Two doctors strapped my arms down straight out each side, and I couldn't help thinking of a crucifixion. They told me it was so I wouldn't grab at them while they were operating, but I couldn't imagine doing that in the first place. Then they raised a blue sheet and blocked my view of what was happening, which increased my fear even more. The pounding in my head grew to a cacophonous beating.

Michael came back and took my hand once more as another doctor began the incision. I couldn't feel the knife, but I could feel the tugging sensation, like someone was yanking my insides. Glancing up, I realized I could see a reflection of the doctor cutting my abdomen in the light above me. I closed my eyes and shivered. Ice seemed to be running through me like a liquid maze.

"We've got a bleed somewhere," one of the doctors said and then the pain exploded in my head. *Was this normal?* I tried to open my eyes, wanting desperately to hear Hope's cry, but the pain became too intense and the world went dark.

"We're losing her." The voice was soft, far away, but I thought it was Michael's. Who were they losing? Me or Hope?

Another voice spoke, even softer, almost like a whisper through a door. "Let's get the baby first, and then we can see what's happening."

There was silence in the darkness, and then the sound of a baby's cry. A peace settled on me, and then the darkness took over.

**

JD and Melanie were still praying when a nurse stepped in the room. "I have some news."

They both glanced up, and JD held his breath. Fear and excitement battled for the dominant emotion in his head.

"You have a daughter, and she looks great. We're going to keep her in the NICU for a few days, but so far we don't see any long term problems. She's 5lbs 5 ounces and 17 inches long."

JD squeezed Melanie's hand and flashed her a tight smile. He waited for the nurse to give an update on Callie and when she didn't, his heart tightened, and he focused again on the woman, whose hands were tightly clasped in front of her.

JD swallowed the lump crowding his throat, "And how is Callie?"

The nurse paused, and her eye twitched as she looked at him. "I'm afraid there was a complication. The doctors are still working on her now."

JD fell back into the chair.

"You can come see the baby whenever you're ready," the nurse offered gently.

"Thank you." Melanie gave her a nod before turning to JD. "God is watching out for your wife now; let's go meet your daughter," she said, touching his shoulder.

JD stared at the change in her. The last two days, Melanie had seemed older, frailer, but suddenly it was like they had switched places, and she was the rock giving him needed strength and support. He accepted the change as he had nothing left at the moment to protest with. Surrendering to the mothering spirit she was offering, he stood and followed her down the hall, but inside he was still numb.

Hope Elizabeth Peterson was perfect. She appeared tiny, but the nurses assured them she was healthy. She had no real hair, but the slightest hint of blond fuzz covered her head, and her eyes were a bright blue.

JD feared holding her at first as the emotions were still battling inside him. One part of him longed to hold her, but another part insisted that it was her fault that Callie was in the situation she was in. That voice began to whisper that this baby wasn't really his and that he'd never be able to love her if something happened to Callie.

JD fought the voice, knowing it was Satan trying to turn him from God's plan. He held out his arms, and the nurse placed the tiny bundle in them. As JD held her, she seemed to look right at him, and then she wrapped her tiny hand around his finger. JD's breath caught in his throat. He wondered again how people could throw these tiny human beings away. Even though she wasn't his by blood, JD knew she was his daughter in every other sense of the word. He reluctantly handed her to Melanie after a few minutes and watched them bond as well.

His fear and anxiety flared anew without Hope in his arms. He needed another way to calm his nerves. "I'm going to go see if there's any news on Callie."

He left the room and headed down the hall to the nurse's station. Callie's doctor stood at the counter conversing with the nurses. As JD neared, he turned, a grim look on his face.

JD's heart dropped. "Is she...?"

The doctor held up his hand. "There was a complication, but we managed to stop her bleeding. Unfortunately, she lapsed into a coma. We don't know why or when she might come out of it, but she is alive."

JD nodded and sank to the floor against the wall. It

wasn't the news he had hoped for, but at least she was alive. He stared at his phone knowing he should text Scott to share the news, but how did you write that the love of your life was in a coma?

A nurse touched his shoulder. "She's back in her room now. Would you like to go see her?"

JD wiped his hand across his eyes and pushed himself up, following the nurse on legs that didn't feel his own.

Callie looked frail and pale under the sheet. JD sat beside Callie and stroked her hand, pushing away the thought of Alexa's death that kept crowding into his mind. "She's beautiful," his voice caught in his throat. "Hope is really beautiful. You did a good thing Callie. Please stay with us. You need to see this beautiful life God used you to create, and she needs to know you. I know that may be selfish, but please God, let her see her daughter." JD put his head down on the side of Callie's bed and wept openly.

CHAPTER 18

When I opened my eyes, I was in my living room. Though everything looked right, something felt wrong. My hands flew to my stomach, but it was no longer large and bulging. It was flat and soft, as if it had never held a baby.

"Hope?" I raced into the guest bedroom that JD and I had turned into a nursery, but it wasn't a nursery; it was still a guest bedroom. The walls were still white, not the lavender JD had painted them for Hope. The roll top desk I had inherited from my grandfather was where the dresser should be, and the black futon couch was in the place of the crib. Clapping my hand over my mouth, my eyes darted around. "What's going on?" Fear massaged my shoulders, and I backed out the room.

Nothing appeared out of place in the hallway, but in the kitchen no sonograms hung on the fridge. I bolted to the bedroom. There was no picture of JD and I on the nightstand, nor was my Bible in its prominent place. The front door lock clicked, and I raced back to the living room.

Rooted to the spot, I watched the lock turn and the door open, and then I gasped. It was Daniel and not JD.

"What are you doing here?"

He glared at me as he threw his coat on the couch and his wallet on the hall table. "Cut the crap, Callie, I live here, remember? Have you been drinking again?"

"Drinking? What are you talking about? I haven't had a drink since I found out I was pregnant."

"Pregnant? Are you pregnant again?" His face flamed red, and he took a menacing step toward me.

"No, when I found out I was pregnant with Hope. You know nine months ago?"

"Who's Hope, Callie?"

"The baby, you know the one you didn't want? The one you said I should abort?"

"You did have an abortion, Callie." He rolled his eyes and plunked down on the couch, as if this was a conversation we had had many times.

"What? No, I wouldn't have. I couldn't have. I mean, I remember going, but then I talked to Sandra, and I decided not to. I remember getting bigger and feeling her move. I saw her ultrasound."

He sighed. "I know; you babble about it nearly every night when you toss and turn in bed. But you did have the abortion and then you changed."

"What do you mean?"

"Look at yourself." He pointed a finger at me, and I looked down. I was standing in a bathrobe. "You quit your job. You stay home and drink all day, and now I honestly think you're going crazy."

"It happened." I sucked in my breath and collapsed in a nearby chair.

"What?"

"I became one of the 80%."

"What are you talking about?" He wasn't listening though; he had picked up the remote and was surfing through channels on the TV.

"You know the 80% that suffer mental health problems after an abortion," I said. "Remember, I told you about these abortion statistics when I didn't want to give up the baby, and you said it wouldn't happen to me. But it did."

"Well whatever the reason, you need help Callie. I won't stick around forever trying to clean up this mess. In fact, maybe I'll go see Shaina." He leaned back on the couch with his hands behind his head and shot me a challenging look.

It should have made me angry, but instead it calmed every nerve in my body. "You probably already have been. I get the feeling you aren't ready to be tied down to just one woman."

"Finally, you understand." Smiling, he planted his feet on the coffee table. "I was so tired of coming up with lies. It really is exhausting, you know? And men aren't meant to stay with just one woman. We need flavors." He resumed clicking the remote. "Now maybe we can work out a plan. Like I spend weekdays here with you and weekends with her or maybe a three-four split? Maybe we can even spend a few nights together with all three of us?"

Swallowing the disgust that rose in my throat, I bit my lip to keep the unclean words I had for him from leaving my mouth. "I've got a better idea." I flashed a tight smile at him. "Why don't you take your stuff and spend every day with her?"

"Be realistic, Callie." He didn't even glance up at me. "You're a mess. I can't leave you here alone."

My eyes narrowed, and I placed my hands on my hips. "I'm going to give you ten minutes, and then I'm going to call the cops."

The chill in my voice grabbed his attention, and he

glanced up. "Look, I'll go tonight, but I'm serious, Callie, you can't be alone, so I'll be back tomorrow and we'll get you some help."

I picked up his coat and wallet and held them out to him. "Leave." The word came out as two syllables, both accented forcefully and with as much hate as I could muster.

"Whatever," he said, pushing himself off the couch. "You're too much work anyway." He grabbed his things and stormed out of the apartment.

As the door slammed shut, I sank down on the couch and covered my face with my hands. I knew this wasn't the path I had chosen, but how did I leave this reality? The silence in the apartment began to close in on me, and I reached for my Bible, only it wasn't on the table. A quick glance revealed it was nowhere in the living room. My eyes darted back and forth as I tried to remember where it might be. Then I remembered where I had found it the first time. Racing back into the bedroom, I bent down and looked on the nightstand. There it was, coated in dust, just as before. As I picked it up, peace flowed through me, but I still had no idea how to get back to the reality I knew. I pulled my cell phone from my pocket and called my mother.

"How long has it been mom?" I asked as soon as she answered.

"Well hi, Callie, how long has it been since what?"

I sat on the bed and picked at the robe. "Since I had the abortion, mom, how long?"

"Nine months, Callie. Your baby would have been born any day now. Are you still having dreams? Is that why you're calling?" My mother sighed on the other end.

"No, or I don't think so anyway. Mom, I'm not supposed to be here or at least not this here. See, I didn't abort Hope. I kept her, but I developed preeclampsia. Something went wrong during the C-section, and I ended up here, but I'm not supposed to be here." The words tumbled out in a rush.

"Callie, I think you are suffering from grief over your choice. Now I love you, but I did not love that decision. I would have loved a grandchild and you robbed me of that, but I'm praying to God to forgive you and you should pray for forgiveness, too. I also think it's time you got some professional help."

My forehead wrinkled, but I stayed silent at my mother's accusation. I had no words to convince her, and I was beginning to be unsure myself. "Okay Mom, I will. Thanks." I hung up the phone and stared at it for a minute. *What can I do?* JD's handsome face popped into my head. He would be able to help me. I punched in the cell number I had long ago memorized and tapped my leg as it rang.

"Hello?" a female voice answered.

My mouth opened and closed, unable to form a word. I hung up the phone and dropped it as if it were a hot coal. Of course JD was with someone. In this reality, the last time he saw me was in the Caribbean with Daniel.

Picking up the Bible, I hugged it to my chest. Now that I had tasted it, a world without JD and without Hope held no meaning. "Is this how it would have been, God? Would my life have been so empty?" I lay back, closed my eyes, and prayed for this nightmare to be over.

CHAPTER 19

*J*D pulled into the church parking lot on his way to his apartment. He hadn't wanted to leave Callie's side, but Melanie had insisted that a) he take a shower and get some fresh clothing at least and b) that he go and see the prayer vigil that Scott had started at the church.

He was amazed by the sheer number of cars filling the parking lot in the middle of a weekday. Locking his car, he stumbled into the building.

Nearly every chair in the sanctuary was filled. He hadn't even known so many people attended their church. Where had they all come from?

"Isn't it amazing?"

He blinked at the sound of Scott's voice and turned to see his friend at the door, Lexi next to him.

"We've gotten so big, we have to be on a rotation basis. We've got local businesses bringing in food as well as a lot of families helping with that."

"Do all these people attend here?"

Scott smiled and shook his head. "No, Sandra organized a lot of this, but when Tony called his pastor friends, several drove over to come pray here. It's amazing. I've never seen a revival quite like this."

"I've never seen anything like this," Lexi said, placing her hand on Scott's arm. A soft pink spread across his face.

"Guess I've missed a lot," JD said, raising his brow at his friend.

Scott put his hand on Lexi's. "Yeah, Lexi accepted Jesus as her savior a few days ago, and we've started seeing each other."

JD wished he were more excited for his friend. Scott definitely deserved it, but a powerful jealousy swept through him. Why should Scott have someone when the love of his life was laying in the hospital, unable to even see her daughter. "That's wonderful," he said, though the words pained him. "I'm going to run home and shower and get back to Callie. I'll keep you posted on any change."

He hurried out of the building before the jealousy made him say something he would regret.

At his apartment, he threw clothes into a bag, then stripped out of his three-day old jeans and t-shirt and stepped into the shower. He turned the water as hot as he could stand it and enjoyed the burning sensation it brought to his skin.

His mind wandered back to Alexa. He had hoped her death would have been the last time he would have to say goodbye to someone in a hospital. She had become addicted to drugs after being diagnosed with cancer. It was how he had started using, partly because she had asked him to do so and partly because he couldn't stand to see her wasting away. The drugs had eased that pain, but only temporarily. When she was gone, even the drugs couldn't quiet the aching in his heart. They had never gotten to have the family he had always wanted, but now he had another chance for that.

JD stepped out of the shower and sighed. This should be the happiest time of his life, and he was happy about Hope. She was like a tiny ball of sunshine. It didn't matter who held her; she always seemed to have a way to touch their heart. But he missed Callie; he wanted her to be able to share in his joy. She had done so much for so many people, himself included, that he couldn't really imagine life without her or life with her comatose. She had to wake up and meet her ray of light. He fell to his knees on the floor, not caring that he was clad only in a towel, and requested God once again heal Callie. This prayer was beginning to feel like a broken record, but he would keep repeating it until Callie woke. After praying, he dressed, grabbed his bag, and then headed back to the hospital.

**

This time when my eyes opened, I was in the familiar field of daisies where a sea of white stretched before me and in all directions. Peace blanketed me as I gazed around. The sun warmed my shoulders, and a light breeze tousled my hair. To the right, a blond baby crawled through a patch of grass, and I knew without a doubt that it was Hope. I called out to her, but the baby didn't seem to hear. I tried to run to her, but I couldn't seem to close the distance.

"She can't hear you," a voice boomed behind me. Turning, I saw a man glowing with an intensity I had never seen before. His eyes were like sapphires, and his blond hair waved gently in the breeze. His white robe was so bright that I had to shield my eyes.

"Am I dead?"

"Not yet."

"Then why am I here?" I motioned to the field around us.

The angel smiled. "Because we wanted to show you something. Something you can take back with you." He waved his hand and thousands of people appeared in the field. There were more people than I could even begin to count.

Furrowing my brow, I shook my head, not getting the connection. "Who are they?"

"They are all those who were saved because of your work and your testimony," the angel replied. "Every one of them would never have been born if it hadn't been for yours and JD's center and even more importantly, your message. You touched the lives of the parents of these people, and they chose life for their babies."

My mouth dropped as I stared in wonder. "But there's so many. I haven't talked to that many people."

"You are not done yet," the angel smiled, "You are only beginning, but there is also a ripple effect. You see this man." He pointed to a man near the front, "This is the son of a high school couple you met and set up with counseling services. She and her boyfriend gave up their sinful ways like you suggested, and because of your message she never went to the abortion clinic, but gave him up for adoption instead.

"And this boy, because he knows he was saved from an abortion, has a passion for saving others – he grows up to be the lawyer who becomes instrumental in finally getting Roe V Wade over turned. That change alone saved millions of lives.

"This one," he pointed to a tall brunette, "is here because of a woman hearing about your story right now. She became a believer because of you, and her daughter will become a neonatal surgeon and save thousands of babies a year.

"And this one," this time he singled out a pretty blond with striking blue eyes, "she grows up to be a medical researcher and discovers the cure for cancer. So do you see now how your words, no matter how small they seemed to you, have a ripple effect you could never have imagined?"

I nodded in awe, still focused on the blond woman who seemed vaguely familiar.

The angel continued, "These people, and others you talked to and will talk to in turn, shared your words and their words touched other people." His hand waved and even more people appeared. "Your world is changing, because of voices like yours. Because Christians are no longer silent, people are starting to turn back to God. You must continue to be a part of that voice. Tell anyone who will listen about the awesome power of the Lord Almighty and stand up against the world for the morals you know are true to God's heart."

I nodded, still trying to take it all in. "I will; I will not be silent. Did you show me the other vision too, the one where my world was different?"

He nodded. "In order to really understand what you had, we wanted you to see where you could have been had your choices been different. Callie, you've had the wonderful opportunity to experience what your life would have been like if you had made the wrong decision at such an important time. If you had chosen the selfish, easy path, your life would not be the same. You would have lost your job, you would have sunk into a deep depression, and you would have died of alcohol poisoning at age 35. Had you chosen poorly, all of them would be gone too."

He waved his hand and the people disappeared, "Your decision to choose Christ and a life for Hope made it possible for their parents to choose life for them as well. Now it's time for you to return to your husband and child – and your mission." He leaned closer and whispered, "Inspire people to righteousness when you go back. Tell them that saving even one life can in turn save millions. Don't let the unborn remain silent."

I stood silent, still overcome by the stark differences he had shown me.

"Now it's time for you to return," he whispered.

"Wait, can I ask for one favor?"

The angel nodded, and I thought of Sandra, who had never gotten to see her baby. I twisted my hands and then peeked up at the angel, "Can I see Isaac? Sandra's Isaac, so I can tell her that he's okay."

The angel cocked his head and closed his eyes. He smiled, nodded, and opened his eyes. With a wave of his hand again, a young man with caramel colored skin appeared before her. He had warm brown eyes and a dimple in his left cheek. He was tall with broad shoulders and kept his hair cropped close.

"Isaac would have been a writer, and he too would have touched many lives, but you can let Sandra know that God has fully forgiven her. She has followed His word and His will since that horrible night, and there's a place for her here when it's time for her to come home. Then, she will get to meet this boy she gave up so long ago."

I tried to memorize every feature of Isaac's face. I was no artist so I couldn't draw him, but I hoped to describe him to Sandra. "Thank you."

He nodded and disappeared and so did the field. I stood alone in darkness unsure of what to do next. Closing eyes, I hoped to wake up in the hospital bed and hold my darling daughter.

As I opened them, I could see my mother sitting by my bed and Sandra a few feet away, gently rocking the baby. I glanced around but didn't see JD. My voice was barely audible as I began to speak. "Hope." I tried again and got a little more volume this time, although it was still barely more than a whisper. "Hope." It was enough for my mother to hear.

"Callie? Oh praise God. She's awake." She leaned over the bed and embraced me. Sandra wheeled closer and brought a sleeping Hope.

My mother helped raise the bed and then handed the sleeping infant to me.

Her face was angelic, and my heart ached with love. "She's beautiful." Tears of joy fell down my face as my entire body tingled in light.

"Yes, she is." My mother touched Hope's cheek. "I know I've told you before, but I'm so glad you chose life for this baby."

"Me too." I picked up Hope's tiny hand and touched her delicate fingers.

The door opened and JD entered the room, stopping short at the sight of me sitting up. "Callie?"

I waved my hand, unsure what to say, and he ran to me, planting kisses across my face. "Praise God." He pulled back and stared at me; then he kissed me again.

"How long have I been out?"

"Three days, honey -- three long days," JD brushed my hair back.

"I missed nearly an entire week of her life?" My heart ached as I caressed Hope's head.

"You did, but think of how many more you'll get to spend with her," my mother said.

Suddenly I thought of Sandra and the pain she must be feeling. "I'm so sorry Sandra, I wasn't thinking."

Sandra smiled, but it didn't quite reach her eyes. "It's okay. I understand how you feel. I'd give anything to see my baby now."

"Oh, I almost forgot. Sandra, I saw him."

"What?" The word came from Sandra, but my mother and JD registered the question on their faces as well.

I smiled, the excitement lighting up my face. "I had an unusual experience while I was unconscious. Mainly I remember darkness, but then I woke up and I was in my apartment, and Hope was gone and Daniel was still there. I was drinking and depressed, and you were with some other woman." I pointed to JD.

"And then I was in a field of daisies, and I saw Hope and an angel appeared. He showed me all the people who were saved through our message, and there were so many. I don't know how we've affected so many. Well, I think some we haven't affected yet, but he said many are affected because of the center, JD." I tried to slow down, but my words tumbled out in a rush.

"Anyway, the angel told me I had to come back to finish the work I was called to do, but I asked him if I could see Isaac first. He agreed, and, Sandra, he was so handsome. He has warm brown eyes and caramel skin and a dimple in his left cheek."

Tears welled up in Sandra's eyes.

"He was so handsome, and I could tell he was very kind. And the angel said to tell you that God forgives you, and when you get to Heaven, you'll get to see him in person." With the words finally out, I took a deep breath and looked from one person to the other.

"Thank you, Callie," Sandra said softly. "That means the world to me."

My mother squeezed my hand. "We should probably let everyone know you're awake now."

"Let's do that in the hall," Sandra suggested. "These two need a few minutes to get reacquainted, and mother and daughter need that too."

The women exited and JD smiled down me again. "I'm

so glad you came back to us and that we will get to be a real family now." He caressed my hair and gazed down at Hope.

"Me too." I touched Hope's tiny hand, marveling at her perfect fingers. "She really is beautiful."

"Callie, I have to tell you something," JD fidgeted with the bed sheet. "I was going to do it before we got married, but then everything happened so quickly and I forgot."

My heart thudded, and a knot of fear developed in my stomach. "What is it? You aren't leaving me, are you?"

"No, not at all." He caressed my arm. "I need to tell you about my past, too."

I could tell that he was troubled by whatever was on his mind. "I'll listen if you need to tell me, but JD, if it isn't who you are today, then it doesn't matter to me. You once told me God would forgive my past when I accepted His son and that lingering on one's past mistakes isn't the thing to do."

"That's true, but I need to tell you in case it ever comes up again in the future."

I nodded, and he continued.

"When I was in college, I met the woman I thought I was going to marry. She was amazing and vibrant and full of life, and she won my heart. What I didn't know was that it was all an act. She had terminal cancer, and she was using some pretty strong drugs in order to appear so happy. We started dating and slowly she introduced me to her drugs. I wanted to support her and so when she offered them to me, I tried them. I must have an addictive personality because I was hooked almost instantly. My life fell apart for a time and it wasn't until she passed away that I realized how far I had fallen. I've been clean for years and have no intention of doing drugs again, but I needed to let you know so you can help me avoid any such temptation in the future."

"Thank you for telling me. I'm sorry you lost someone

you loved. The fear of losing me must have been hard for you when I was comatose."

"Yeah, I can't say I'm a big fan of hospitals. Speaking of which, when can we leave here?"

Laughing, I kissed him again. I couldn't wait to get home either.

CHAPTER 20

*A*fter amazing the medical staff with my quick recovery, we left the hospital a few days later - as a family, and headed home.

JD carried Hope's car seat into my apartment. "I guess I can start moving some of my things in here now, huh?"

"Oh my, we didn't even think about that." I laughed as I realized all the changes I would need to make. "I'm going to need to make some room in my closet."

"It's okay. I didn't bring that much with me, but we're going to need to discuss whether we plan on staying here or moving to New York."

His words gave me pause. I hadn't even thought about that when I had accepted his proposal. I had been so excited, but Texas was my home, and I couldn't imagine Hope growing up in New York. My gaze traveled to the floor, and I bit my lip. How could I tell him I didn't want to leave?

"Don't worry," he said, touched my arm, "We'll pray about it."

I nodded and picked Hope up from the car seat, settling

her against my chest. As I carried her around the apartment, I pointed everything out to her.

"And here's your room." Pink and purple flowers and butterflies adorned the lavender walls, along with the wooden letters H O P E. Hope smiled and yawned, so I laid her down in the crib and left the room.

JD's arms enfolded me as I stepped into the living room. It was a tight, secure feeling that I had missed. When he released me, he moved his hands to my face. "Are you okay for a bit if I go and grab a few things from my place?"

As much as I wanted him to stay, I was tired myself and looking forward to sleeping in my actual bed.

JD rubbed his thumb over my lip and then followed it with a soft kiss. "I'll be back as soon as I can."

As he left, I crawled into bed and closed my eyes. I didn't regret having Hope for a minute, but I hadn't realized how tiring being a new mother would be.

❀

*J*D climbed in his rental car. Now that Hope was here, and Callie was awake, there were a lot of things they had to figure out. Even if they stayed in Mesquite, they would need a bigger place soon and a bigger car. JD didn't really miss New York, but he did wonder what would happen to his father's business if he left the running of it up to others. Could he manage it long distance? He did have the board members, and they had been running everything anyway. JD sighed. He had always thought getting married would make things easier, but it came with its own challenges. He prayed for clarity for all the decisions he would have to make as he drove to his apartment to pick up a few things.

He'd already packed a few pieces of clothing when he

had stopped by earlier, but he took his time this time grabbing his shaving equipment, toothbrush, hairbrush, and essentials. He added a few dress shirts and pants that he could wear to work at the center and then loaded up his car.

❀

*J*D was making dinner when I woke later. He stood in the kitchen, cradling Hope in one arm while he stirred a pot of soup.

Yawning, I issued an apology. "I'm sorry, I didn't even hear her cry."

"No worries. She's been great. She helped me pick out all the vegetables." He smiled as he tickled her under her chin.

"Is there anything I can do to help?"

"Not me, but you might want to check your messages." JD pointed a spoon to the machine. "I didn't feel like it was my place yet, and I'm pretty sure they're all for you anyway."

I wrapped my arms around him and kissed his cheek. "For future reference, my messages are your messages, but thank you."

As I pushed the button on the machine, I was surprised by the number of messages from friends who had been praying and then calling to congratulate my recovery.

Tears formed in my throat. "Wow, it never ceases to amaze me how many people were praying for me."

"You've been quite an inspiration to many people." He set a bowl down in front of me. "And I hope you don't mind, but a few of them wanted to throw you a baby shower. I told them this weekend would be fine."

"That's sounds great." The vegetable soup he set down looked warm and inviting.

"I've been praying, too." JD set his bowl down and then sat across from me, still cradling Hope. "You've got roots here, and I've started to put them down as well. I want to continue to see the center grow. The Board has been running my company the last few years anyway, so I'm starting to feel like God is moving me here."

Joy filled my heart. I hadn't even wanted to think about moving to New York, though I knew I wanted to stay with JD wherever he was led.

"I'd like to pray about it some more, but would you be opposed to staying here?"

I shook my head, my grin reaching from one ear to the other. "I would have gone where ever God led us, but I can't tell you how happy I am that we are getting to stay here. I can't think of a better place to raise Hope."

❀

J smiled at the gathering of people in our living room the following weekend. Mine was not the typical baby shower, but I wouldn't change it for the world.

My mother had arrived with a man, and she seemed happier than I could remember her looking in years. I'd have to ask her about that new relationship when I could. It was true I had been busy the last few months, but it was unlike my mother to keep something that big from me.

Lexi and Scott had shown up together. JD had informed me that not only had Lexi had accepted Christ, but that the two were now dating. I smiled at that answered prayer.

Sandra, of course was there, chatting with some of the girls from the center. Evidently, she had stepped in to help at the center while JD and I were at the hospital those five days. Though we had an office manager, I knew that Sandra had a place at our clinic as well, and I couldn't wait to discuss the idea with JD. The group was rounded out with Tina and a few other friends from church.

"Well," Melanie began, "thank you all for coming. Obviously, the baby is already here." Everybody smiled at Hope who was fast asleep in my arms, "but we thought this would also be a great time to get together and celebrate Callie's return to us."

A round of clapping ensued. "Of course, we did bring some things for Hope." Melanie picked up a present.

I stood and crossed to Sandra. "Will you hold her for a minute while I open them?" Hope already had a special place in Sandra's heart.

Tears dotted Sandra's eyes. "Of course," she held out her arms.

I returned to my chair and began opening the gifts and displaying them to everyone.

After all the gifts were open and the food was eaten, everyone packed up and left except for my mother, who was helping clean up, Tom, who was chatting with JD since my mother was his ride, and Sandra. Sandra wheeled over to the rocker I was sitting in, rocking Hope.

"I wanted to say thank you." Sandra touched my arm.

"For what?"

She grabbed the bag off the back of her wheelchair and pulled out a rolled piece of paper. As she unrolled it, a gasp escaped my lips; the face of Isaac looked back at me.

"Did you see him?"

A soft smile tugged at her lips. "Is it him then?"

"It's perfect." My fingertips grazed the portrait.

"I used to draw a long time ago, and when you told me about Isaac, I knew I had to try to draw his portrait. I used your description and an old picture of Peter, his father, and myself. I was hoping I'd get it close to the real thing."

"You got it spot on." I squeezed Sandra's arm.

"Thank you for asking to see him and for giving me the description. I'll be ready to meet him when Jesus is ready for me, but until then I now have something to look at. I can never thank you enough, Callie."

"I'm so happy I could help you, and I'd also like to ask you to be Hope's godmother. She is going to need strong female role models, and I can think of no one else I'd rather have."

Sandra's eyes filled with tears, and she nodded her agreement. She said goodnight, took her picture with her, and headed home. Melanie and Tom left soon after, and I laid Hope down for a nap.

"Callie, I know we're officially married," JD said, hugging me, "but I feel like we missed out on having a real ceremony at our church. When I get back from New York in a few days, would you like to try again to have a real ceremony?"

I smiled up at him. "I'd love that, though I'm starting to wonder if I have bad luck with weddings." We both chuckled, and then I leaned against JD's chest, enjoying the security he exuded.

❀

*J*D landed in New York the next afternoon and took a taxi to his office. He had already finished the lease on his apartment months ago before he left, but he needed to hire a moving company for all the things he had placed in storage. Then he needed to tell the board members he was planning to stay in Texas. "Lord, give me the strength and the energy for this."

He climbed the stairs to his office, opened the door, and crossed to his computer to find a moving company. That needed to be his first job so that the movers could be packing up his storage unit while he did everything else. Once he had that lined up, he went looking for the board members.

When the majority of them were assembled, JD cleared his throat and wiped his palms on his pants. "So, I thought I'd give you an update on the center in Texas. Faith Pregnancy Center is up and running. We're starting rather small, but the word is getting out there and people are coming in. Of course, that's not why I asked you to meet me here today. I wanted to tell you that I'm not coming back to New York. I'll be checking in with you all every other week through video conferences, but I'm going to be staying in Texas to run the center and be with my family.

"We sort of expected as much." Fred nodded and pointed to JD's left hand, "Especially when we noticed that ring on your finger."

Relief flooded JD, and he told them all about Callie and Hope.

❀

One month later, I stood in front of the mirror and stared at my reflection. My brown hair was pulled up, and a few curly tendrils hung down barely touching my cream-colored dress. I thought back to the last time I had stood in front of a mirror like this and shook my head at the difference. Life hadn't turned out the way I had planned.

I was still losing the baby weight from Hope, so I wasn't at my ideal weight yet, but I didn't care. Junior Partner was never going to happen, but I felt more fulfilled helping JD at the center and sharing my story with the women who came in. As I usually had Hope with me, the little girl had also begun her own career in affecting others, even though she didn't even know it. I had, however, married a handsome, rich man, (though not for those reasons) and today I was going to get to have the ceremony I had dreamed of. My only hope was that it went off without a hitch, unlike last time.

A knock at the door interrupted my thoughts, and I turned as Lexi, my mother, and Tina entered the room.

"Are you almost ready, honey?" My mother asked.

I smiled and nodded. "Is everything else ready?"

Lexi nodded. "Yep, JD is standing at the front waiting for you, along with Scott. Sandra has Hope in the front row, and the food all got delivered on time and it looks delicious."

"The cake?"

"Yes, it's here and looks great," Tina said.

"Okay, well then I guess I'm ready."

I smoothed my dress one more time and then followed Lexi, Tina, and my mother out to the hallway. Lexi and Tina had both agreed to reprise their roles as bridesmaids and, to cut down on cash, they were wearing the same gowns they had worn last time. The bouquets were each new though, beautiful bouquets of lilies and carnations. My own bouquet was made up of fire and ice roses and pink carnations. Tina and Lexi opened the doors to the sanctuary and paused before beginning their march down the aisle.

As the doors closed again, my mother turned to me, pulling me in for a hug. "I'm so proud of you; you've grown into a better woman than I even could have hoped."

"Thanks Mom." I squeezed her back, "I'm thankful you never gave up on me."

"Moms don't give up on their children, ever." She wiped the tears in her eyes, and then turned to open the doors.

The music began, and all eyes turned toward me. I glanced to the front of the church where JD stood, smiling at me and handsome as ever in his tuxedo and pink tie. Taking my mother's arm, I marched towards him, glad to be feeling no pain this time.

At the end of the aisle, my mother hugged me one more

time and then went to sit next to Sandra, who was cradling a sleeping Hope.

Pastor Tony smiled and addressed the small crowd. "Thank you to everyone for joining us once again. Hopefully, we have no unexpected interruptions this time."

Hope took that moment to let out a large wail, and a laughter scattered through the sanctuary.

Tony continued the vow renewal ceremony, finally pronouncing us husband and wife again.

The crowd cheered as JD leaned in and placed his lips on mine.

When the kiss ended, we walked hand in hand down the aisle, past our many friends and family. Yes, this wasn't the perfect day I had once pictured for myself – it was even better.

HE END

*I*f you enjoyed this book, please keep reading for a special sneak peek at When Hearts Collide.

DISCUSSION QUESTIONS

1. What do you think the theme of this book is? What's the message the author is trying to get across?

2. What was it about JD that finally made Callie start seeing the issues in her life?

3. Who was your favorite character in the book and why?

4. Why do you think Callie gave Daniel a second chance after his betrayal?

5. What Sandra does every day take a lot of courage. What could you do that would be courageous for God?

· · ·

6 . What did you learn about God from reading this book?

7 . How can you use that knowledge in your life from now on?

8 . Is there something you could do at your church to help inform or love on women in this position?

9 . What are you looking forward to about Heaven?

1 0. Who are the three main victims of abortion?

*F*ear covered Jared like a blanket. The music that had been uplifting now pounded a drum of dread in his heart. Why did it have to be so loud? He pulled desperately on the arm of a nearby boy, spilling some of his beer. "Where's Amanda?" The boy rolled his eyes, cursing a little at his spilled beer, and shrugged Jared off.

Jared turned to another, who gave the same response. His heart pounded like a freight train as his eyes tore wildly around the room. He had known this was a bad idea. Frat parties were often dangerous, this one even more so.

The crowd of bodies pressed against Jared, surging to the beats of the pulsing music. Sweat from those around him joined his own, trickling down his back. He pushed against the crowd, fighting his way to the other end of the house where the bathroom and bedrooms lay. He had to have taken her to one of them. A hand grabbed Jared's wrist, and he whirled on a blond surfer type with long hair.

"Sorry, bro," the surfer dude said, holding his hands up in apology.

Jared continued toward the back. A tipsy blond fell into

him, and he shoved her to the side. The bathroom door loomed just ahead.

"Amanda?" Jared pounded on the white wooden door. "Amanda, open up if you're in there." The pounding of his heart was now reverberating in his head, creating a headache that made his eyes hurt.

The lock clicked, and the door opened. A thin brunette in a miniskirt and crop top stumbled out. "There's no Amanda here." Her words were a slur, and her brown eyes barely focused on him.

Jared grabbed the girl's thin shoulders and shook her. "Have you seen her? Red hair? She would have been with Caleb West."

The girl shook her head and fell into the wall as soon as Jared released her. Rolling his eyes, he pushed past the girl and opened the first bedroom door. A couple was entwined on the bed, but the girl had blond hair and the face of the man didn't belong to Caleb.

"Sorry," He pulled the door shut and moved on the next one. Another couple was heavily involved on this bed too, but again no Amanda.

The next door was locked. This had to be the one. Jared rattled the handle, but to no avail. "Amanda?" He pounded on the door, but he heard no noise from inside. Jared grabbed the arm of a nearby male and pointed at the door. "Hey, can you open this? Do you have the key?"

"Sorry, I don't live here." The man shrugged and walked away.

"Aargh!" Jared turned back to the door and rammed his frame into it. The door didn't budge. Perhaps a kick would work. He took a step back and planted a perfect front kick. He felt the reverberation up his leg, but not even a tremor from the door. Cursing under his breath, Jared looked around for anything to wedge in the door. Would they have a crowbar in the house? Would anyone have one in their car?

"Jared!" At the sound of his name, Jared whirled around. Emily was fighting her way to him through the crowd. Thank goodness, she had seen the text. A glance at his watch revealed ten minutes had passed since he had texted her when he'd first lost sight of Amanda.

"Have you seen her?" Emily asked when she reached him.

Jared shook his head, the fear constricting his vocal chords. "Not since I texted you. I saw them at the punch table and then a friend came up to me and started talking. When I turned around again, she was gone. It's my fault."

"It's not," she said, running a hand through her long blond hair. "You warned her, and that was all you could do."

Jared wasn't sure about that. He should have pushed harder. He should have told her the whole story and not just part of it, but none of that made a difference right now. Right now, he needed to find her. "I've already checked those two rooms," he said pointing to the previous doors, "but this one's locked."

Emily glanced around, but like Jared, her search came up empty. "I'm assuming you already tried hitting the door," Emily said, "but what if we tried together?"

"It's worth a shot," he said. "On the count of three, okay?"

Emily nodded, and on the count of three, they both rammed the door as hard as they could. This time the wood did tremble, but the door remained locked.

"Again," Jared said through clenched teeth, and together they rammed the door once more. This time a wonderful terrible splintering sound of wood echoed, and the door opened. Jared rushed into the room.

Amanda lay sprawled on the bed. Her shirt was open and her pants were undone, but still on.

"Check on her," Jared yelled to Emily as he scoured the room for any sign of Caleb. The closet was empty, but a chill crept in from the open window. Jared stuck his head out, but the area was dark and devoid of movement. If Caleb had gone out this way, he had gotten enough of a start to be out of sight. Without knowing which direction he had gone, trying to follow him would be pointless.

With an agitated sigh, Jared turned back to the bed. Emily had wrapped the comforter around Amanda, whose eyes were wide open and filled with fear.

"Can you move?" Emily asked. No head shake, but Amanda's eyes moved left and then right. "Okay, it's going to be okay. We'll get you out of here. Any sign?"

"No, the window is open, but he's gone." A tear slid out of Amanda's eyes. "Don't worry, we'll find him. He won't get away with this." Jared patted her hair tenderly and wiped the tear from her cheek. Then he scooped her up and headed back out the door. "Let's get her to the hospital."

"An ambulance is on its way," Emily replied, pocketing her cell phone.

Jared nodded as he pushed his way through the crowd. A few people turned to gawk at them as they made their way to the front door, but most were oblivious and kept dancing to the loud beats or tipping back their drinks. Jared shook his head as disgust boiled inside him. What was wrong with these people? Did they not even care that someone had been attacked?

The night air slapped him as they exited the stifling house, and the change in temperature sent a shiver down his spine as the cool air licked up the wet sweat dripping down his neck.

The ambulance roared up moments later. The EMTs

climbed out and took Amanda from Jared, strapping her onto a gurney. As they loaded her into the back, Jared climbed in.

"There's only room for one," the EMT said as Emily attempted to climb in too. "Besides, the cops want a statement." He pointed to the police car pulling up.

"Go. I'll stay with her, and when you're done, we can switch," Emily said.

Jared nodded and mouthed a silent thank you to Emily as the doors closed. He grabbed one of Amanda's hands and sent a prayer heavenward. *Please God let her be okay, please God.* He had no other words, and hoped God was hearing his heart, which felt like it was beating out of his chest. Though he'd only known her a few months, Amanda was a friend, and if he were honest, he hoped she would become a lot more.

When the ambulance braked, Jared fell forward a little. Chilly air rushed in as the back doors opened and doctors took over the gurney Amanda was on. Jared jumped down from the ambulance and hurried to keep up with them.

"Amanda? I'm Dr. Patrick, can you tell me what happened?"

"She can't," Jared spoke up. "I'm pretty sure she was drugged."

The dark-haired doctor turned to him. "And you are?"

"I'm Jared. I'm a friend, and I found her. Her eyes were open and seemed responsive, but she couldn't even shake her head."

"Okay, we'll take it from here. You can wait over there." He pointed to the waiting area. Jared wanted to protest, but he could tell from the look in the doctor's eyes that his protest would fall on deaf ears, so he nodded and stumbled over to a gray, vinyl chair. As he sank down, the weight of the night descended on his shoulders, and he dropped his head onto his hands.

He hadn't been able to stop it. Was this what Nikki had gone through? Was this why she left without a word? Would Amanda do the same thing?

"Hey, are you okay?"

Jared jumped at the touch to his shoulder ready to lash out at the intrusion, but relaxed when the eyes he saw belonged to Emily. "Yeah, I guess I'm alright. How are you?"

Emily sighed as she sat next to him and pulled her knees to her chest. "I've been better. They asked me a lot of questions. I couldn't answer most of them, so they'll be looking to talk to you too. But I told them what little I could. How is she doing?"

"I don't know," Jared sighed. "They whisked her away pretty quickly and haven't been back out yet. I'm worried, Emily."

"I am too," she said with a nod, "but the best thing we can do right now is pray." She took his hand, and they closed their eyes. "Father, our friend Amanda needs your help right now. Please be with her and give the doctors the knowledge to treat her. Lord also help us know how to help her in the future."

As they said amen, Jared added a silent plea for Amanda to be okay. If she wasn't, he wasn't sure he'd ever be able to forgive himself.

 urchase When Hearts Collide to continue reading.

WOULD YOU LEAVE A REVIEW?

As an author, I highly appreciate the feedback I get from my readers. It helps others make an informed decision before buying my book. If you enjoyed this book, please review at your retailer.

Do you like free books? I'm offering a free sample of my next book Free Sample!

REFERENCES

References and Resources

1. State / Church FAQ *Freedom From Religion Foundation* January 6, 2016.
   <://ffrf.org/faq/state-church/item/21714-religious-and-freethought-clubs-in-public-school>
2. THE HOLY BIBLE, NEW INTERNATIONAL VERSION®, NIV® Copyright © 1973, 1978, 1984, 2011 by Biblica, Inc.® Used by permission. All rights reserved worldwide.
3. ProtestPP.com
4. LifeNews.com
5. Prolifeaction.org
6. Online for Life app now called Human Coalition
7. Abolish Abortion app
8. AfterAbortion.org
9. http://www.teenbreaks.com/abortion/abortiondoctors.cfm
10. Prolife.com
11. http://www.dailywire.com/news/3654/abortion-

doctor-explains-just-what-abortion-its-amanda-prestigiacomo

12. http://www.aaplog.org/pregnancy-resource-centers/

13. www.oregonlifeunited.org/

ABOUT THE AUTHOR

Lorana Hoopes is an inspirational author originally from Texas but now living in the PNW with her husband and three children. When not writing, she can be seen kickboxing at the gym, singing, or acting on stage. One day, she hopes to retire from teaching and write full time.

ALSO BY AUTHOR

If you enjoyed this story, be sure to check out Lorana's other books.

When Love Returns
    Once Upon a Star
    Love Conquers All
    Where It All Began
    The Power of Prayer
    When Hearts Collide
    A Past Forgiven
    The Billionaire's Secret
    Brush with a Billionaire
    The Billionaire's Christmas Miracle
    The Billionaire's Cowboy Groom
    Lawfully Matched
    Lawfully Justified
    The Scarlet Wedding
    Lawfully Redeemed
    Lawfully Pursued
    The Still Small Voice
    Love Renewed
    When Love Returns
    Once Upon a Star
    Love Conquers All
    The Cowboy's Reality Bride
    The Reality Bride's Baby

Her children's early reader chapter book series:
The Wishing Stone #1: Dangerous Dinosaur
The Wishing Stone #2: Dragon Dilemma
The Wishing Stone #3: Mesmerizing Mermaids
The Wishing Stone #4: Pyramid Puzzles
The Wishing Stone Inspirations #1: Mary's Miracle
To see a list of all her books

authorloranahoopes.com
loranahoopes@gmail.com

www.ingramcontent.com/pod-product-compliance
Lightning Source LLC
Chambersburg PA
CBHW031133210626
46816CB00014B/702